FORESTS

of the NIGHT

FORESTS
of the NIGHT

A Johnny Hawke Novel

DAVID STUART DAVIES

Thomas Dunne Books

St. Martin's Minotaur

New York

THOMAS DUNNE BOOKS.
An imprint of St. Martin's Press.

FORESTS OF THE NIGHT. Copyright © 2005 by David Stuart Davies. All rights reserved. Printed in the United States of America. No part of this book may be used or reproduced in any manner whatsoever without written permission except in the case of brief quotations embodied in critical articles or reviews. For information, address St. Martin's Press, 175 Fifth Avenue, New York, N.Y. 10010.

www.thomasdunnebooks.com
www.minotaurbooks.com

Library of Congress Cataloging-in-Publication Data

Davies, David Stuart, 1946–
    Forests of the night / David Stuart Davies.—1st U.S. ed.
        p. cm.
    ISBN-13: 978-0-312-36000-9
    ISBN-10: 0-312-36000-2
    1. Private investigators—England—London—Fiction. 2. World War, 1939–1945—England—London—Fiction. 3. London (England)—History—Bombardment, 1940–1945—Fiction. I. Title.

PR6104.A857 F67 2007
823'.92—dc22

                                                      2006049781

First published in Great Britain by Robert Hale Limited

First U.S. Edition: January 2007

10 9 8 7 6 5 4 3 2 1

This book is dedicated to two wonderful women:
in memory of my dear mother, Alice, who introduced me
to the world of books, and to Kathryn, my rock,
my inspiration and my love.

Tyger! Tyger! burning bright
In the forests of the night,
What immortal hand or eye
Could frame thy fearful symmetry?

William Blake (1757–1827)

prologue

My career in the army was very short but far from sweet. As a young policeman with 'considerable prospects', or so my sergeant told me, I was reluctant to leave the force and join up, but I was idealistic and patriotic and, if I'm honest, in search of adventure. 'Thank God, you're going,' Sergeant Brannigan said with a friendly pat on my back, the day I told him that I had enlisted. 'I'm too old myself and with you out of the way I can be sure I can hang on to my stripes. You give the Hun what for, eh?'

I didn't give the Hun what for. Not in the way Brannigan intended at least. I got no further than Aldershot. Something cropped up that changed the course of my whole life. It was December 1939, two days before Christmas, when it happened. I was on the rifle range learning the intricacies of how to fire a rifle with a modicum of accuracy. The officer in charge, Sergeant-Major Stock, was not one given to careful instruction. When patience and coherence were being handed out, he was lagging behind being fitted with an enlarged voice box. No doubt as he emerged from the womb he had given the midwife an ear bashing about her sloppy performance. Such was the nature of the red-faced incompetent in charge of firearms training. As a result, the young novices under his command may as well have been looking down the wrong end of the barrel for all the clear instruction that was given. But to be fair to the large-gutted bully, he really had nothing to do with what happened to me. It could have been any one of our company. It just turned out that I was the unlucky one.

We queued up and Sergeant-Major Stock, like a rifle

monitor, doled out the weapons from a large wooden box. They all looked the same but unfortunately, there was some obstruction lodged in the barrel of the one I was given. I didn't know this until I fired the gun and it exploded in my face.

It was as simple as that.

There was a dull explosion and for a moment the world turned a brilliant white like a fierce polar landscape. It was dazzling in its intensity. A sudden, stabbing, violent pain shot up my arms and across my chest and I felt a blast of searing heat on my face as a vivid flash filled my vision. I thought my head would explode. Then I lost consciousness.

When I woke the world was in darkness. A velvet black inkiness pressed down upon my eyes. My throat was dry and my head throbbed like a road drill. I could tell that I was lying in a bed but that was all. It took me quite a time to recollect anything. Gradually I managed to piece fragments of my recent memory together. I heard the explosion and saw the sheet of yellow flame and remembered the pain.

I called out for help. And within seconds I felt the cool touch of a woman's fingers on my arm and a sweet voice saying, 'Welcome back to the land of the living.'

I half smiled, but it soon disappeared from my lips. Strangely, it took me a few moments to realize that I couldn't see her, this woman who had come to my aid. And yet my eyes were open. What had happened? I felt my body grow tense with panic. Once again I recalled the explosion and the bright searing heat. My God, I thought, I am blind.

'I can't see!' I cried, struggling to sit up.

Those cool hands held me back.

'It's the bandages,' she said. 'You have bandages on your eyes. You have been badly burned, Johnny.'

Johnny. She knew my name.

'Who are you? Where am I? What's wrong with me?'

She chuckled gently. 'Questions, questions. You are in Aldershot General and I'm Nurse Watkins, Jenny to you.'

'And what's wrong with me?'

There was a pause before she replied. 'There was a nasty firearms incident. On the shooting range. Remember?'

I paused a moment to reassemble the memories. 'I remember – but what's the matter with me?' I had gained more power in my voice and my question was brusque and urgent.

I felt her palm smoothing my brow. 'You need rest now,' she said, avoiding the issue. 'The doctor will explain everything in the morning.'

'Can't you take the bandages off? I want to see.'

'Not yet, Johnny. We must wait for the doctor. You really should get some rest.'

She squeezed my hand and then I heard her leaving the room.

How could I rest with so much uncertainty hanging over my head? I wanted to know the extent of my injuries. Why was the lovely Nurse Watkins – and to me her voice pronounced that she was lovely – so circumspect about my condition? Despite my worries, fatigue rolled in like a large breaker and swamped me. Soon I was carried away on the sea of sleep. As I drifted into unconsciousness, I was aware of voices singing. A Christmas carol. A radio maybe, or a choir of angels....

The next day I was roused briskly and breakfasted on a weak porridge mixture – it was spooned into my mouth – by another nurse, who was businesslike and impersonal, before I was visited by the doctor – Doctor Moorhouse. He was far from circumspect.

'You're a lucky man, Hawke,' he announced, as though he were addressing a class of medical students. 'You could have had your head blown off – a rifle exploding in your face like that. Count yourself fortunate that you're still here to tell the tale.'

'What tale can I tell?' I asked, not wishing to discuss with him his rather twisted definition of 'fortunate'. 'What's the matter with me? Tell me straight, Doctor, am I blind?'

He gave a gentle laugh. It was unnatural, forced. An embarrassed laugh. He'd told me why I should be thankful to be alive before he dropped the bombshell. That was his bedside manner.

'Well?' I prompted, pulling myself up in bed as best I could, angry now at all his prevarications.

I felt the doctor sit down on the edge of the bed. He sighed. 'You're not blind, Mr Hawke. You will see again. But I'm afraid that you have lost your left eye. The heat of the explosion....'

I can't remember any more of what he said. My mind just blanked it off. The shock and pain of his revelation shook me physically. My body shuddered and I started to sweat. Instinctively my hand went to the accursed bandages. I wanted to rip them off and prove this damned quack wrong.

I didn't, of course, because deep down I knew that he must be speaking the truth. Why would he lie? I had lost an eye! I was a cripple. A disfigured cripple. I was only twenty-five. Young. Not yet had a serious girlfriend. And now I never would. I was a leper. A disabled freak. Johnny One Eye. At that moment, I wanted to die.

LONDON

1940

one

He pulled the thin, single sheet over his head and curled his body up into a tight, foetal position. It was as though he wanted to squeeze himself into nothingness. He shivered not because he was cold but because he was frightened. Frightened of so many things. He prayed that he wouldn't wet the bed again.

The light was on in the other room; yellowness seeped in through the crack along the bottom of the door. And there were voices: his mother and a man. Another man. It was never the same man. It was the usual nightly performance. He had no watch but he knew from experience that it must be somewhere around half-past eleven. The pubs had closed and they'd come back. Despite his youth, he knew what they had come back for. He'd glimpsed it one night when his mother had been moaning so much that he'd thought she was in pain. He'd walked in and found them on the rug by the fire. There was this large black man lying on top of his mother. They were both naked. He was panting and sweating and she was moaning as if she had tummy ache.

That night he learned that it was true, the stories he'd heard in the playground about men and women.

Sometimes the men were violent. More than once his mother had a black eye in the morning and on one occasion she had a cut lip. She always shrugged off her injuries as 'the risk of the job' and assured him as she ruffled his hair, if she was in a good mood, that the odd bruise often brought in some extra cash.

Every night he lay awake waiting, praying for it to be over. In fact, the silences were the worst: lying in the dark, wondering if it was finished for this night, or whether it was merely an interval before it started again. Sometimes the men stayed all night, but as soon as they saw him in the morning, they scuttled off pretty sharpish, carrying an air of guilt with them. Some of them wore uniforms but they behaved no differently from the rest. In Peter's eyes they were all animals. And so was his mother. He knew that God expected him to love his mother and he had tried to – but he couldn't. He knew that mothers smacked their children when they were naughty but he was never deliberately naughty and yet she beat him. Especially when he wet the bed. 'You can't love someone who doesn't love you back,' he explained to his pillow, his eyes moist with frustration.

Then he heard his mother's raised voice. 'You'll bloody pay me anyway. It's not my fault you can't get it up. You'll bloody pay me for my time.' Her words were slurred and delivered in a hysterical tirade.

'Like hell I will,' the man rasped back at her. 'How d'you expect me to get aroused with an old tart like you? I'd rather shag a keyhole.'

'You bastard,' she screamed, and there was the sound of a scuffle. 'Give me my bloody money.'

'Don't get clever with me, lady.'

There was the noise of something crashing to the floor.

Peter leapt out of bed, tiptoed across the cold linoleum and opened his door slightly so that he could see into the room.

The body of his mother, dressed only in her underclothes, lay on the rug before the fire. Her eyes were closed and she was not moving. Standing over her was a tall, dark-haired man who was pulling on a sweater over his head. His movements were awkward and slow. The man picked up his jacket from the settee and then turned once more to the boy's mother. 'You fucking old tart,' he said, kicking her in the ribs. She did not respond but lay very still.

The man leaned down until his face was within inches of hers. 'D'you hear me, you old tart? I'd rather fuck my mother than come anywhere near you.'

Somewhat unsteadily he crossed to the door and, slamming it heartily, he left.

Peter waited for some moments before he emerged from his bedroom. He wanted to be sure that the man had really gone. Crossing gingerly to his mother, he knelt down by her side. Already her bloated face was starting to bruise. As he leant his head towards hers, he could smell the stale alcohol on her breath.

'Mam, Mam,' he cried shaking her. 'Mam, Mam, are you all right?'

There was no response.

'She's dead,' he told himself in a terrified whisper. Tears welled up in his eyes. 'Oh, Mam.'

He fell on her, his head buried in her bosom as he sobbed for the loss of the mother he didn't really love.

Then suddenly, she stirred. The eyes opened lazily, the pupils rolling erratically.

'What the bloody hell...?' she muttered thickly. 'What the hell d'you think you're doing, you little bastard?'

Peter jumped up in shock, a mixture of relief and despair. 'Mam, you're alive.'

His mother raised her head slightly. ''Course I'm fucking alive. More's the pity. What the hell to do you think you're doing, crawling all over me? Get out of my sight, you little sod. God, I wish the midwife had drowned you at birth. You're nothing but a fucking nuisance. Get out of my sight. Go on, get out of my sight, do you hear me? I never want to see you again.' She slumped back, the outburst draining the last drops of energy from her, and she slipped once more into unconsciousness.

'I never want to see you again.'

The words seemed to echo round the tawdry room. They thundered in his brain. Peter looked down at the pathetic creature sprawled on the rug in front of him. What had the man called her? An old tart? Suddenly a new emotion entered his consciousness, causing his young body to tremble. It was anger. It was hot-blooded resentment against the woman who had ill-treated him for so long. Now he hated her, really hated her, hated her with an overwhelming fervour. He kicked her just as the man had done. 'You old tart,' he cried, mimicking the man. 'You're not my mother,' he added, his voice strong and devoid of emotion. 'You're not my mother.'

Yet again her words came back to him, 'I never want to see you again.'

Peter turned and walked back to his own room. He knew what he had to do and he was fearless in his decision. He dressed quickly and then, wrapping up some underclothes and a couple of shirts in some newspaper, he placed them in a carrier bag. He came back into the living room on tiptoe. His mother was still unconscious, but now she was snoring, her mouth agape and her tongue lolling to the side. Peter searched for her handbag and found it on the floor by the settee. Tipping out the contents, he picked up his mother's purse. There was little cash in there, but he took a ten-shilling note and five shillings in smaller coins and slipped them into his raincoat pocket.

Clutching the carrier bag, he made for the door, his heart beginning to pound. Now he was close to leaving, to making the big break, he prayed that his nerve wouldn't fail. He turned back to look at his mother, his eyes moist and his hands clenched.

'I never want to see *you* again,' he said softly and then ran from the room, leaving the door ajar.

t w o

I spent the afternoon at the pictures. Well, someone has to keep the fleas company and there's quite a colony at the old Astoria. I think I am probably at my happiest, sitting in the dark amid a scattering of silhouetted strangers watching some flickering fantasy up there on the silver screen. I suppose it is an escape route from reality, from the war and my own cock-eyed, one-eyed existence.

On leaving hospital after my 'firearms incident', with a small cheque as compensation for my injuries and a regulation black eye patch, I found myself adrift. Stamped disabled, I was no longer eligible for the army, well, the fighting army at least. I was told that they could find me a nice little safe clerical job somewhere. When I turned the offer down, I think they were relieved. I was an embarrassment to them – a reminder of their incompetence. It was the same story with my old employers, the police. They couldn't have a one-eyed copper chasing a couple of burglars down the high street. He might let one of them escape.

So what was a young red-blooded cyclops in search of some adventure in his life to do? Well, I know what *I* did. I used my compensation money along with my savings to set up as a private detective in London. If I couldn't be an official copper, I'd be an unofficial one and utilize what skills I had developed while I was in the force. I rented two rooms in Priors Court, an ancient block of flats at the north end of Tottenham Court Road; one was my office and the other was where I ate and slept. I shared the bathroom with other members of the motley crew who had found themselves washed ashore in the same building. And so Hawke Investigations came into being.

Any dreams of excitement and danger living the life of a private detective soon evaporated. At first no one came. I became a candidate for winning the world's thumb-twiddling championship. Then slowly I began to receive a trickle of clients: angry husbands and wives wanting proof that their partners were dipping their spoons in someone else's teacup and a few credit companies employing me to seek out their defaulting debtors who had run to ground. It was hardly Bulldog Drummond but it kept a roof over my head, which is more than some of the poor devils in the East End could say, courtesy of Herr Hitler's Luftwaffe.

As bleak autumn turned to harsh winter in 1940 the work began to dry up, hence my trip to the cinema. I had to pass my time somehow. The womb-like darkness of the picture palace helped for a time to mask those realities that I wished to forget. While scores of young men my age were actively fighting – and, indeed, dying – for their country, undergoing all kinds of hardship and deprivation, here I was living a comparatively comfortable life faraway from the front line. I felt guilty. The guilt was exacerbated by the fact that my brother Paul was out there somewhere 'giving the Hun what for'. And here was I sliding down in a cinema seat, puffing on a Craven A, waiting for the big picture to start. The truth was that I hated myself. I hated myself for only having one eye.

For the next ninety minutes I joined Tiger Blake in yet another of his 'rip-roaring adventures'. This time he was in search of *The Lost City*. Tiger had been a childhood hero of mine. I first encountered him as a comic strip in my boys' paper and then he emerged as a film star. There had been at least a dozen Tiger Blake movies and I'd seen them all. They had taken me from puberty, through my teenage years and here I was at twenty-six still following Tiger's exploits. The series was now rather old hat. Budgets had been cut, the sets were wobblier and it seemed to be on its last legs. The star, Gordon Moore, who had been in his mid-thirties when he'd played the part for the first time in *Tiger Blake and the Devil's Doorway*, was now approaching fifty and, I'm afraid, he looked it. His hair was obviously thinning and his once slender, muscular shape was running to fat. To make matters worse, his leading lady was significantly younger and resembled his daughter rather than his love interest. Nevertheless, I enjoyed the movie. It wasn't very good but it had a strange nostalgic appeal to me and for a short time I was transported back to my worry-free early teens when I wanted to be Tiger Blake, the man who, with one bound, was always able to break free from every tight corner in which he found himself. Paunchy, balding and slower in the action scenes than he had been, Tiger was still my man.

I left before the newsreel. I can't bear to watch scenes of the war. In that respect I was a coward, I suppose, but I knew it would only increase my sense of frustration and despair.

It was dusk and a thick fog had settled down on London. Pulling up my collar and tipping my hat forward, I headed for Benny's Café on Dean Street. As I walked, I glimpsed dimly-lighted shop windows through the shifting grey curtain of fog, while pedestrians, unidentifiable dark shapes, slid silently by. It was a good night to be anonymous.

Soon the bright window of Benny's Café beckoned like a beacon.

'So it's Sherlock Holmes.' Benny gave me a wave as I entered. 'How's business?'

'What business?'

'That bad, eh?'

I nodded and took a seat by the window. It was approaching seven o'clock, closing time, and I was his only customer.

'Today's special is Brown Windsor Soup, and Shepherd's Pie.'

I shrugged. 'That'll be fine,' I said, lighting up a Craven A. Food only interested me when I was happy, otherwise I saw it merely as a fuel to keep the body going. I dug into my pocket and dragged out some change. I was running low on funds. In my current financial circumstances that trip to the flicks had been an extravagance. Not only would horns have to be pulled in, but hooves and tail, too.

Benny was not the best of cooks – the soup tasted of gravy browning, which it probably was, and no self-respecting shepherd would have touched the pie, not even with his crook – but Benny was a friendly soul and I felt at ease in the place.

As I chewed on the strange brown stringy material that lay beneath the crusted layer of potatoes, I glanced up and saw a face staring in at me through the condensation-bleared window. It was a young face, a pale mask that bore a haunted look. A boy, somewhere around ten or eleven years old. The wide eyes stared at my plate enviously.

I smiled back at him. The face froze for a moment in fear at being seen and then vanished from sight. I went to the door and looked out. He had gone. I could hear the boy's running footsteps disappearing into the distance as tendrils of fog enveloped me.

three

After I'd finished what I could of Benny's repast, he cleared the plates away, raising an eyebrow at my leavings. 'You'll never build your strength up if you let good food go to waste,' he said. I bit my tongue – which was somewhat more tasty than the pie – and nodded. Locking the door and switching the Open sign around to Closed, Benny came and sat beside me and offered me a cigarette.

'You look as though you've just had an appointment with Mr Hitler himself,' he observed, blowing smoke over his shoulders. 'Such a face.'

I grinned. 'Nothing so exciting.' I was used to Benny mother-henning me and I didn't mind. In fact, it was quite touching.

'Tell me, Johnny, what would bring a smile to that so unhappy mush of yours? What do you need? Mind you,' he added, waving his arms in mock horror, 'if it's cash, you've come to the wrong fellow. Shepherd's pie and Brown Windsor soup don't make a man rich. If it did, Buckingham Palace I would live.'

I shook my head. 'No, it's not cash.'

'So ... what? What do you need?'

I took a deep drag on the weedy little cigarette and let the smoke escape slowly until it almost masked my face. 'A purpose,' I said.

I left Benny's about half an hour later and wandered around the fog-enshrouded West End for best part of an hour until inevitably my feet led me to The Velvet Cage, my second home. It was a jazz club run by a somewhat dodgy Greek character called George Cazmartis. I'd done a job for him when I first started up as a private detective. Someone was regularly dipping his fingers into the till and I'd been able to ram it shut while the hand was still there. Not exactly a pivotal moment in the history of crime detection, but it had impressed Georgie so much that he had given me life membership to the club. I could get in free anytime I liked. And I liked. It was on a par with the cinema: a dark, smoky place where one could be anonymous.

I nodded to Charlie the doorman and passed through the swing doors. Immediately I could feel the heat of the club waft towards me as though it was desperate to escape the stifling, hazy atmosphere within. It was an atmosphere I loved: the jazzy, boozy world where one could slip into veiled anonymity and soak up the pleasure.

I was just in time to catch Tommy Parker's first set with a new singer, Beulah White, who sang like Billie Holliday's sister but looked like her mother. She warbled 'I loves you Porgy' with such sweet power that I found my eye moistening. The honeyed voice with the gravelly undertone soothed and elated and like all good singers, touched the soul. After she'd finished, I dug deep into my fading resources and bought her a drink and we fell into talking about songs and how to sell them. She believed that clichés in the lyric weren't necessarily a hindrance as long as the melody was strong enough to compensate. 'A good tune gives added depth to the words. 'You listen to what I do with 'Love for Sale' in the second set,' she grinned, her white teeth illuminating her care-worn face. I raised my glass in toast to this as she excused herself to 'powder her nose'. Judging by her raddled features and dreamy eyes, I reckoned this was a euphemism for some other activity in which powder and her nose would feature.

'Johnny. Good to see you.'

Without turning, I knew the voice. It belonged to a little fat man in a double-breasted dinner suit which was two sizes too small for him and the possessor of a nose so hooked he could have gone fishing with it. It was the owner, Georgie the Greek. I turned and gave him an insincere smile.

Casting his beady eye on my empty glass, he beckoned to the barman. 'Jimmy, give Mr Hawke a Scotch on the house. A double.' He grinned his benevolent grin, his lips almost stretching round to touch his nose. Patting me on the back once more, he evaporated into the crowd to practise his benevolent mine-host act elsewhere. As I lifted my refreshed glass and inhaled the whisky fumes, I wondered why, despite his generosity to me, I didn't like the man. What the hell, I liked his whisky, especially when it was free.

Beulah's singing was more erratic and less assured in the second set. She certainly lost her way through 'Love for Sale', although I could see what she had been aiming for. It was clear that she was at her best before she powdered her nose.

I stayed on at the club until just after eleven, buying myself another double Scotch. My pockets now had lost their chink. As the crowd began to thin out, I decided to add to the process and make my way home.

The fog had cleared considerably, just leaving behind phantom wisps of grey that floated like ectoplasm on the stiff November air. Junior ghosts on their way home. The streets were empty and, as I walked along, I was accompanied by the clip clop of my own footsteps. I began to feel a little guilty now at leaving the office unattended for most of the day. It would be just my luck if I'd missed some rich client, or better still some exciting case, with a missing diamond and beautiful blonde – the sort that Tiger Blake gets. At the thought of my hero Tiger Blake, I grinned an inane, inebriated grin.

I was about two streets away from Priors Court when, as I passed a darkened shop doorway, I heard a noise emanating from the blackness. It was the sound of crying. Gentle, stifled sobs in the shadows. Breathing in the cold night air to help clear my head, I investigated.

As I moved nearer to the doorway, the sobbing stopped abruptly and there was a frantic scrabbling sound like some animal in distress. In the gloom I could make out the shape of a young boy cowering in the corner, his knees bent up to his chest and his face turned into the corner, hidden from view as though he was desperately trying to make himself invisible.

'Hello,' I said softly.

As soon as I spoke, the youth gave a cry of alarm, scrambled to his feet and rushed forward in an attempt to push by me. I side-stepped so that he ran straight into my arms. He gave a shriek of terror and kicked me on the shin. I winced but hung on.

'Let me go. Let me go,' he yelled, as he wriggled furiously in a desperate attempt to escape my grasp.

'Whoa,' I said quietly, but holding him firmly. 'Just stop your struggling, sonny. You're not going anywhere.'

He kicked me again and although it was quite painful – painful enough to make me mouth a silent swear word – I held on to the boy.

'Look,' I said, 'you might as well give in. I am bigger and stronger than you and I'm not going to let go.'

Slowly the boy relaxed his efforts and slumped like a puppet with its strings cut. 'Don't hurt me, mister,' he said softly. 'I'm doing no harm.'

I led him from the shadow of the doorway towards the light of a street lamp. He was dressed in short trousers and a dark belted raincoat. His hair was ruffled and his features tear-stained and grimy. I'd seen him before. This was the spectre at the feast – the haunted face that had stared at me through the steamy window of Benny's Café.

'What are you doing out at this time of night on your own?'

The boy averted my gaze and said nothing.

'Where do you live?'

'I ... I haven't got a home. I don't live nowhere.'

'What about your parents?'

'I got no parents. They're dead. Both of them ... dead.'

Now he started to cry and without embarrassment he clung to me and sobbed. I didn't know what to think. Parents or no parents he had come from somewhere. It was clear from his appearance that he had not been living rough for long.

'I'm Johnny. What's your name?'

'Peter.'

'Peter what?'

'Just Peter.' He wasn't going to be caught out like that.

'Well, Peter, my lad, you can't sleep in that doorway all night, that's for sure. You'll catch your death in this weather. You'd better come home with me.'

To my surprise the lad offered no resistance to this suggestion. I reckoned that he was too weary to object. I took his hand in mine and we walked down the empty street looking for all the world like father and son returning home from some event – a party or a trip to the cinema. I thought it best not to pressure him with questions about his home and family. I needed to let him learn to trust me a little first. It was clear that for whatever reason he'd done a bunk. Maybe his parents were really dead and he had scaled the walls of the orphanage to explore the big wide world, or he'd been farmed out to some strict spinster in the country and he'd skedaddled back to town but was now too afraid to face his parents. I'd find out in due course. After all, I was a detective.

For a brief moment I remembered my own longings to leave the orphanage. How sometimes I'd get up in the middle of the night, clamber on to a chair and stare out of the window. When the moon was bright I could see the trees and fields beyond the confines of Brookfield House. That was the real world – the world of mums and dads and houses and hugs and kisses, birthday presents and laughter. I never did anything about 'escaping'. It was just a dream – but when I talked about it, my brother Paul, who was a realist, told me not to be so stupid. He knew that I wouldn't find what I longed for. There was a completely different life agenda for orphans.

'When was the last time you had something to eat?' I asked, as we approached Hawke Towers.

The boy shook his head. 'Dunno. I had some choc'late this morning.'

I grinned. 'Well, let's see what I can rustle up.'

Not much is what I could rustle up. The Hawke larder is on a par with Old Mother Hubbard's. However I did possess a rather rusty tin of Spam and some baked beans – not exactly cordon bleu but as I prepared this midnight feast the boy's eyes lit up with excitement. He sat on the sofa, still wearing his grubby raincoat and watched with fascination as I prepared the food – lighting the gas ring to warm the beans and unkennelling the spam.

The food was wolfed down in minutes.

'You enjoyed that, eh?'

He nodded shyly. 'Thank you, mister. Can I go now?'

'Go where?'

The boy pursed his lips. He had no answer.

'Another doorway somewhere, eh? I have a better idea – you kip down here on my sofa tonight. It's a bit lumpy but it's a damned sight more comfortable than stone flags. How about that? No strings attached.'

The worried eyes looked uncertain but the temptation of somewhere warm to curl up overcame his misgivings.

I grabbed the eiderdown from my bed and flung it at him with a smile. 'OK, Pete, you make yourself comfortable and get a good night's sleep. And remember, no snoring.'

For a moment that weary tear-stained face lost its frown and the ghost of a smile touched his lips.

Within minutes he was curled up in a tight ball on the sofa, almost lost under the eiderdown, and purring gently as he sank into deep and, I hoped, untroubled sleep.

four

The boy slept soundly for two or three hours and then a disturbing dream brought him savagely awake. He had been running down a long, featureless corridor, but no matter how hard he tried he could not shake off the dark, hooded figure that was chasing him. Indeed, the figure was gaining on him. Then Peter tripped and fell and the figure loomed over him, its darkness seeping outwards ready to envelop the boy.

Gasping for air, Peter sat up, his chest heaving silently as he tried to contain his panic. For a moment he didn't know where he was. The shadows in the room were alien to him and then he remembered. The strange man with the black eye patch and the warm food. As he shifted his position, he felt the dampness between his legs. He had wet himself again. He bit his lip in shame and sorrow. He had thought that in leaving his mother, he would never do that again. Now he would smell of wee and everyone would know he was 'a fucking bedwetter'. He sniffed back a tear. He would not cry. All that baby behaviour was behind him now that he was a grown up, alone in the world.

Gradually his eyes became accustomed to the gloom and he was able to make out the features of the room. To his dismay he saw that the man with eye patch was slumped in the chair by the fireplace. He was fast asleep, his head lolling back and his mouth wide open. Every now and then a gentle guttural snore escaped from the gaping aperture. The man had been nice to him, but he knew that sooner or later he would try to take him back to his mother and he didn't want that. He had to escape.

Carefully, so as to make no noise, he pulled back the eiderdown and collected his shoes from under the sofa. He tied the laces in a simple bow – the only way he knew how – and stood up. He spied his raincoat hanging on the back of a chair by the window. Like a character in a film shot in slow motion, he crossed the room and retrieved it. He had no idea where his carrier bag was but there were only a couple of shirts and a couple of pairs of underpants in it anyway. He would have to leave it. He couldn't risk waking the eye patch man.

Then he spotted the man's jacket lying on the table. Peter felt in the inside pocket and pulled out a wallet. It contained two one-pound notes only, some stamps and a few receipts. Taking one of the pound notes and slipping it into his trouser pocket, he returned the wallet. He didn't like the idea of stealing, especially stealing from a man who had helped him, but in the short time Peter had been on the streets he had learned that he had to be practical rather than sentimental. And anyway, he hadn't taken both pound notes – he had left one.

Slipping the latch up noiselessly, the boy let himself out of the room.

The sky was still black as Peter emerged once more into the cold November night. He could grab a few more hours' sleep in a doorway somewhere before it was light. Then he'd go in search of a place for breakfast with his newly acquired wealth.

five

When I awoke, the miserable grey light of dawn was already forcing its miserable way through the miserable crack in the curtain and illuminating my miserable dump of a room. My tired, drink-befogged brain had rested while I slept but was still only functioning in first gear as I regained consciousness and it took me some time to recollect the circumstances leading up to me kipping down in the armchair instead of the lovely lumpy bed in the alcove. Ah, yes, I told myself, as I rubbed my prickly chin and blinked my good eye: the boy. I sat up, yawned and gazed over to the settee, expecting to see Wee Willie Winkie cradled in the arms of Morpheus. But of Wee Willie Winkie there was no sign. The eiderdown was on the floor and the settee was vacant. The lad had done a bunk. What a fool I'd been not to lock him in. He was a fugitive after all. I pictured that small, gaunt face with the haunted eyes. He was running away from something or someone and was terrified that I'd take him back. So terrified that he'd wet my settee and then gone back to a life of cold doorways and scrabbling for food.

Well, I'd done my best. Well, the best I could muster after a long day and several whiskies. What the hell, it really was no concern of mine. This thought had hardly entered my mind before I rejected it. I hadn't done anywhere near my best and it *was* a concern of mine. I swore and then put on the kettle. A mug of scalding tea and a cigarette would civilize me and sharpen the brain. My pal at Scotland Yard, Detective Inspector David Llewellyn, might be able to help. He certainly would be able to provide me with a list of any dark-haired boys of about ten years old who had been reported missing in the last week. By the state of Peter's coat (if Peter was his real name, of course), he'd not been living rough for more than three or four nights. And then I could do the rounds of the down and out shelters along the Embankment and see if I could pick up a scent. Well, I'd be guaranteed to pick up a scent mixing with the army of the great unwashed. What I meant was a clue. At least it would give me something to do. A purpose.

I sat at the table, pouring the hot tea down my throat, wondering where the poor blighter was now. However much that little bastard voice at the back of my mind tried to deny the fact, I was involved and I had to do something about it.

Ah, but it's the way of the world: when one makes definite plans, something crops up to disturb then. By 9.30 I had got myself washed, dressed and presentable. With a smooth but slightly bloody chin courtesy of a geriatric razor blade, a clean collar round my neck and two slices of toast within me, I was feeling almost human again and ready to make my way to Scotland Yard when my office doorbell rang.

That could only mean one thing: I had a client. Or clients to be precise. There were two of them: a middle-aged man and woman. They stood on my doorstep, side by side as though they had fallen off a shabby wedding cake. They introduced themselves as Mr and Mrs Palfrey – Eric and Freda. If I were a film director shooting a sequence where I needed a dull, middle-class couple in their late forties with precise manners and limited imagination, Mrs and Mrs Palfrey would be ideal casting.

The matter was obviously urgent. One could tell that by the way Mr Palfrey gripped his rolled umbrella, trying to strangle the furl and Mrs Palfrey tapped her nails on her shiny imitation crocodile-skin handbag.

I sat them down in my office, while I perched above them on the edge of my desk. 'How can I help you?' I said, smiling benevolently.

'I'm afraid our Pamela is absent without leave,' said Eric Palfrey with a nervous grin, staring at me through a pair of spectacles borrowed from Arthur Askey. He had a precise manner of speech as though he had rehearsed his lines several times before spouting them.

My smile turned to a puzzled frown. 'I'm sorry...'

'What Father means,' interrupted Freda Palfrey, 'is our daughter Pamela has left home ... is missing. She's been gone two months now.'

Left home. Who could blame the girl? I was already beginning to feel edgy with the Palfreys and I'd only been in their company for a few minutes.

'How old is your daughter?'

'She is twenty-seven,' said Father, as though describing the blackest sin in the Bible. His tone and the curl of his lip suggested that to be twenty-seven and female was the equivalent of being a brothel keeper in either Sodom or Gomorrah – or both.

'Has there been a row? Did she leave because of some disagreement?'

'No,' said Mr Palfrey.

'Yes,' said Mrs Palfrey, the drumming nails now reaching a frenzied crescendo.

I stared at them blankly.

'Well,' said Mr Palfrey, 'I suppose it depends on how you define a row or disagreement.'

'How do you see the matter, Mrs Palfrey?' I asked, ignoring Father for the moment.

'Pamela had a perfectly good job working as a typist for a very nice solicitor in Bermondsey, but her head was always filled with film star rubbish. All her free time was spent at the pictures or reading those terrible film magazines. She was besotted by it all. She got it into her head that she wanted to work in films. But we told her it wasn't a respectable occupation for a young lady.'

'Certainly not,' snapped Mr Palfrey. 'These film people are not our sort at all. They're rather common individuals leading shallow and tawdry lives.'

I nodded sympathetically.

Mrs Palfrey continued, 'Then Pamela came to know this girl... Samantha. I don't know her last name. We never met her. Apparently Samantha worked at Denham Film Studios in the offices and she would fill Pamela's head with all sorts of nonsense about what goes on there. How glamorous it all was. How she had met this film star and that one. Poor Pamela became obsessed with the idea of working there, too.'

'When we put our foot down, she walked out on us.'

Good girl, I thought. At twenty-seven you deserve a little freedom and self choice. The idea of the straight-laced Palfreys putting their collective foot down together created a comic cartoon image for me and I had difficulty in suppressing a smile.

'So,' I said, after lighting up a cigarette, 'what I think you are saying is that Pamela has left home with the idea of getting a job at Denham Studios and perhaps has gone to live with her friend, Samantha.'

Mr Palfrey nodded firmly. 'That was our understanding – but there are certain problems.'

There usually are, I thought. 'Go on.'

'We thought at first that she'd come back pretty sharpish after realizing what life is like without a loving home to come back to. But she didn't. So last week I contacted the personnel department at Denham Studios to see if they have employed a Pamela Palfrey recently and they say that they have not.'

'She might have used another name.'

'I suppose it's possible. But they also told us that they don't have anyone called Samantha on their staff either.'

Now it's beginning to sound like a case, I thought. 'Have you informed the police?'

'Oh, no,' cried Freda Palfrey, her fingers flexing themselves for another riff, 'we don't want to get the police involved. It makes it seem like a criminal matter. That's why we've come to you. At heart, she's a good girl. We just want her home again.'

Eric Palfrey nodded vigorously. 'Freda would just like us to wait and pray and hope everything will be all right, but I think we must be doing something more active. I can't just sit at home not knowing where she is and how she is. I've told her we must take matters into our own hands. That's why we've come to you. We want you to find our daughter, Mr Hawke. We want to know that she's safe.'

I nodded. 'I can try. There are no absolute guarantees in this business, as I'm sure you appreciate, but I will do my best.'

Mrs Palfrey started to sniff and dabbed a lace handkerchief to her nose. Mr Palfrey leaned forward in a stiff manner and patted her on the shoulder in a consoling way. 'Take heart, Mother. I am sure Mr Hawke will get to the bottom of the mystery.'

'Do you have a picture of your daughter?' I asked, interrupting this intimate moment between Mother and Father.

'I thought you'd need one, so I brought two,' Mr Palfrey replied, extracting two sepia snapshots from his wallet and passing them to me. They showed a very plain and rather podgy girl in a loose dress, wearing the same kind of owlish glasses as her father. Her hair had been curled in such a manner that it appeared to be escaping from her head. There was a strange sadness about the eyes which indicated that she knew fate had dealt her a cruel blow. She looked like a cow's bottom and she could never demonstrate the beauty she felt inside.

'They were taken last summer in our back garden. I would say that she's lost a little weight since then,' chipped in her mother, the sniffling done and handkerchief squirrelled away somewhere.

'Apart from this Samantha, Pamela had no other friends? A boyfriend perhaps?'

'Apart from Clark Gable, Errol Flynn, Robert Donat, Gordon Moore and chaps of that ilk, no,' said Mr Palfrey, in an attempt at bitter irony.

'And you've no idea where this Samantha lives or what she looks like?'

The Palfreys shook their heads.

'You'd better give me the address of the solicitor where she used to work. I might be able to pick up a lead there.'

'I thought you'd need that,' grinned Mr Palfrey, and once again he opened his wallet to extract a postcard with the solicitor's name and business address copied out in neat black writing.

I grinned back, but my heart and my lips weren't in it. 'Very organized, Mr Palfrey. Thank you.'

'I try to be. You will also find our address and telephone number on the back of the card. I have spoken to Mr Epstein on the telephone – that's Pamela's old boss – but he wasn't able to help us. He was as much in the dark as to her whereabouts as we are.'

I nodded sympathetically. 'I have to ask you this. Supposing I find your daughter but she doesn't want to be found? Hard as it might be for you to contemplate, it is possible that she does not want to return the warm bosom of the family. She might be perfectly happy where she is now.'

This stopped them in their tracks. The possibility that dear Pamela had sloughed off her parents' restraints and lifestyle for good had not crossed their tiny, tidy minds.

Eric Palfrey shifted awkwardly on the chair. 'I ... I am sure,' he said, tartly, 'that whatever dream world Pamela hoped to find out in the ... big world will have proved more than disappointing – disheartening even – and she'll be more than willing to come back to Mon Repos.'

'Mon Repos?'

'The name of our house.'

I nodded. Of course. They would be the kind of people who give their little middle-class home a name to distinguish it from Dun Roamin next door or Bide A Wee over the road. Even this strike at individuality had a staleness and a predictability about it. Surely it would be a sin to return podgy Pamela to the shackles of this arid environment. I wondered if in some other office in another part of London another set of distraught parents were begging some reluctant private investigator to try and find their missing boy, a little, dark-haired chap called Peter. Somehow, I doubted it.

'If you take on the case, Mr Hawke, we'd be happy to pay your fees in advance.' Mrs Palfrey opened her handbag and tugged at a large brown envelope inside. 'Our savings. Anything for our little girl.'

I felt a pang of guilt for being so dismissive about their feelings, their mutual despair. It seemed that whatever passion had brought them together thirty years ago had shrivelled and all they had left in their arid little lives was their daughter. But instead of allowing her to grow and develop, they had hemmed her in, trying to fashion the girl into the creature they wanted – probably a mirror image of themselves.

'That won't be necessary,' I said, more quickly than I intended. 'If you can give me twenty pounds to start with to cover my immediate expenses, we'll take it from there.'

Mrs Palfrey nodded and lowered her head. I thought she was going to start crying again. Instead she pulled out four five-pound notes from the bulging envelope and placed them on my desk.

With as much encouragement as I could muster I bade my new clients farewell for the moment, assuring them that I'd be in touch within a few days. Left alone in my office, I felt empty somehow. I knew that solving the task they had set me would bring misery to one or possibly both parties. Not a happy prospect and not much of a job for a man to do. With a sigh I scooped up the five-pound notes and folded them into my wallet.

six

Peter stared at the garish poster outside the Astoria cinema.
There was excitement and glamour in its gaudy colours and
crude images. He ran his fingers gently over the shiny surface,
stopping now and then when he reached a ripple where the
paste had dried in a lump. It was a pleasing sensation. *Tiger
Blake and The Lost City* the poster said. 'Starring Gordon
Moore' it also said in big letters; and then underneath in
smaller letters it said: 'with Peggy Crawford, A. Bromley
Davenport and Freddie Forbes. Directed by Norman Lee.' And
then in giant letters across the bottom, it screamed: ALL NEW
THRILLS. The picture on the poster depicted Tiger Blake, a
younger and more athletic version than the actor who played
him, clinging to a jungle vine with his right hand, a large dagger
in his teeth and a pretty blonde woman held in the crook of his
left arm. In the background there were some ancient stone huts,
which Peter thought must be part of the 'Lost City'. It was all
so wonderful.

Peter wanted to be like Tiger Blake: brave, strong and free.
And always having exciting adventures. What had been a desire
to see the film when he first came upon the poster had now
developed into a raging passion. He needed to see *Tiger Blake
and The Lost City* as though his life depended upon it. But it
was an 'A' picture and he knew they wouldn't let him in on his
own. If he went to the pay box the lady behind the glass would
just turn him away. He glanced up at the frosty-faced lady
ensconced in her kiosk, filing her nails. She certainly didn't look
the kind who would make any concessions to him.

He was well aware that he was too young to see an 'A' by

himself. He had to be accompanied by an adult. However, this shouldn't present too much of a problem, he thought. He'd done it before. You just needed to be a little brave – like Tiger Blake.

So Peter loitered by the entrance to the Astoria. It was early afternoon and business was slow. Of the few patrons that passed him none seemed suitable for his needs. Then he spied a potential saviour. A tall, thin, elderly man with half-moon spectacles and what Peter thought was a kind face. As the man passed him, Peter tugged at his raincoat.

''Scuse me, mister, will you take me in with you? I've got the money.' He held out some coins on the palm of his grubby hand to demonstrate his veracity. The man caught off balance by this unexpected encounter, looked bewildered.

'I just want to see Tiger Blake,' said Peter, earnestly, his eyes pleading. 'Please.'

The man smiled and nodded. 'So do I. All right, give me your money then.'

Peter passed over the coins and accompanied the man to the kiosk.

'One and a half stalls, please.'

The bored woman in the kiosk passed over the tickets without a glance at the boy.

Within moments Peter was in the darkened auditorium where a flickering shaft of light from the projector caught numerous trails of cigarette smoke as they floated up towards the ornate ceiling. On screen Laurel and Hardy were trying to push a piano up a long flight of steps. The soundtrack was noisy and shrill.

'Thanks, mister,' Peter whispered to the man who had acted as his passport to this make-believe world and then he hared off down the aisle.

Peter sat three rows from the front where, to his delight, the screen almost enveloped him. He scrunched down in his seat with his knees pressed up against the one in front. He was in heaven. He didn't care much for Laurel and Hardy. He thought they were too slow to be funny. He much preferred The Three

Stooges with all the silly noises when they hit each other – which they did a lot. But he was content to watch Laurel and Hardy for the moment for he knew that before long he would be accompanying Tiger Blake in search of The Lost City.

After Laurel and Hardy had completed their task with the usual disastrous results, the lights came up and there was an interval. Peter resisted the temptation to buy an ice cream. He realized that he had to watch his money very carefully and one luxury in a day was enough. He wished now that he'd taken the other pound note from that one-eyed bloke's wallet.

Eventually the lights dimmed and with a gentle rattle the curtains swept back to reveal the screen again. To the accompaniment of dramatic native drumbeats the titles appeared: 'Gordon Moore as Tiger Blake in *Tiger Blake and The Lost City.*'

In the warm dark, Peter slowly left reality behind. There were no more thoughts of his mother, of cold doorways, wet beds and the bleak unfathomable future; he was in the steamy African jungle on safari with his hero, in search of German spies who had stolen some secret plans. He was happy.

seven

I met up with David Llewellyn, my tame Scotland Yard chum, for a lunchtime drink in The Guardsman, a cosy pub not a dart's throw away from the Yard itself.

I'd been involved in a murder investigation before the war when David had been the officer in charge. Despite the difference in our ranks – I was a mere police constable then – we had hit it off and formed a friendship which survived the vagaries of my career. If the truth be known, we had little in common apart from liking a drink and a passion for detective work, but that was sufficient in these ragged times to maintain a friendship. I knew I could always rely on David if I needed a bit of official help with an investigation.

'What is it this time?' he asked, after downing a third of his pint in one gulp. Before I could reply, he wagged a finger at me. 'Now don't deny it. You want something from me. You never invite me out for a pint unless I can be of service to the great detective.'

'It's a reciprocal process,' I grinned.

'Hey, don't you use such big words with me. I'm just a simple lad from the valleys with only a school certificate to my name.'

'You get a pint and I get some information.'

'Just one pint, is it?

'Maybe two. Depends on how co-operative you are.'

He grinned. 'That's better. OK, old son, what's the pitch?'

I told David all about my encounter with the boy Peter.

'The poor bugger,' he said, when I'd finished. 'Sadly it's not a unique case. The truth is that there's a lot of young 'uns living rough these days. What with the little devils orphaned by the bombing ... and then there are those who do a bunk because they don't want to be evacuated. It's a shitty old world if you're a youngster at present.'

I nodded in agreement and ordered another pint for my thirsty companion who had just drained his glass.

'Certainly, I'll check for you but I don't hold out much hope. A dark-haired lad about ten or eleven in a blue raincoat, possibly called Peter. Not much to go on there.'

'I know. But somehow I feel responsible ...'

'Responsible? How?'

'I'm not sure. I shouldn't have let him escape, I suppose.' I shook my head. 'I can't explain it.'

'You are going soft in your old age, my son.'

'Maybe. Anyway, let me know what you can.'

'Will do. And you must come round for a meal with Alice and me some night. You're looking peaky. One of Alice's meat and potato pies will take some slack off your belt.'

'That would be good,' I said, knowing that it would never happen.

It was the middle of the afternoon by the time I got to Bermondsey south of the river and the offices of Leo Epstein, Solicitors. They were up a rickety staircase above a shoe-repair shop. I tapped on the door and entered a reception area which housed several filing cabinets and two desks. One desk was empty, the typewriter shrouded in its black cover, but a dark-haired girl was seated at the other desk sifting through some sheets of paper. She looked up and smiled. 'Good afternoon,' she said, her smile broadening. She was very pretty.

'Hello,' I said, returning the smile and removing my hat. 'I'd like to see Mr Epstein.'

'Do you have an appointment Mr ...?

My name is Hawke, John Hawke. No, I don't have an appointment. Is that a problem?'

'I shouldn't think so. What shall I say you want to see him about?'

Before I could reply, the door of the inner office opened and a thin, dark, good-looking man with a shiny bald head and keen features came halfway into the room. This I deduced was Boss Man, Leo Epstein. I judged that he was in his early thirties and yet his manner and bearing were those of a much more mature man. On seeing me, he smiled too. It was a practised, professional smile. 'Good afternoon,' he said.

I nodded.

'This gentleman, Mr John Hawke, wishes to see you, Mr Epstein,' said the pretty girl.

'Ah,' he said, as though she had explained something very revealing about me. 'What is the nature of your business, Mr Hawke?'

'Pamela Palfrey.'

At the mention of the girl's name his brown skin paled. The veneer of his supreme self-confidence cracked a little. 'What exactly ...'

'In your office, eh?' I suggested.

Epstein hesitated for a moment and then held his door open for me to enter. In comparison with the bare and utilitarian outer office, his domain was luxurious: thick wool carpet, mahogany desk, velvet curtains and a very nice-looking drinks cabinet. From the swift manner with which he ushered me to a chair and swept past the cabinet, it was fairly clear that I wouldn't be offered a snifter. No doubt drinkies were reserved for wealthy clients of which, no doubt, there were a few.

'I am a private detective, Mr Epstein.'

Mr Epstein raised an elegant eyebrow. I am sure that he'd seen enough private detectives in his line of work to have deduced that for himself. We carry a certain shabby aura with us.

'I have been employed by Mr and Mrs Palfrey to locate their daughter, Pamela. They've lost touch with her.'

Epstein nodded but said nothing

'As I understand it, until recently she worked for you.'

Epstein nodded again and steepled his fingers together. But the lips remained closed.

I persevered. 'What do you know about her disappearance, Mr Epstein?'

He shook his head. 'Nothing.'

So it was like that, was it?

'Now, that can't be absolutely true, Mr Epstein, and as a solicitor I am sure that you will be fully acquainted with the concept of absolute truth.'

'I know that she handed in her notice about a month ago and I haven't seen her since. I thought it was unusual and somewhat abrupt but employing young typists is a risky business. They are always leaving, moving to live nearer their boyfriends or getting themselves pregnant or married.'

'Why not employ older typists then?'

Something I'd said really tickled Epstein's fancy, so much that he chuckled. 'Well, one likes to see a pretty face around the place. I am sure you know what I mean.'

I pursed my lips. 'I am sure I do know what you mean Mr E, but Pamela Palfrey was hardly a pretty face, was she?'

It was Epstein's turn to look bewildered. 'If you say so, Mr Hawke,' he said softly.

'Did Pamela give a reason for leaving? *She* wasn't pregnant or getting married, was she?'

'Good gracious, I think not. She just told me that she'd found another job with better pay.'

'Where?'

'She didn't say and I didn't ask. I do not pry into the private lives of my employees.'

'Weren't you curious?'

'Why should I be?'

I shrugged.

Suddenly, he leaned forward over the desk. 'Look, I told all this stuff to her parents when they came round here quizzing me. Quite honestly, with a mother and father like that I don't blame the girl for doing a disappearing act.'

He sat back, his moment of earnest revelation over. His face slipped into an impassive mode once more.

'Did she speak of her parents?' I asked.

Epstein shook his head.

'Do you know of her friend, Samantha?'

Another shake of the head. 'I can assure you that I know nothing of Miss Palfrey's personal affairs.'

'I see you haven't replaced her yet.'

'I'm interviewing some girls tomorrow.'

'Pretty ones, I hope.'

'What do you think?'

'Well, I won't take up any more of your valuable time, Mr Epstein, but I'll leave you my card in case you remember anything that might help – or indeed if Pamela gets in touch.'

Epstein took my card as though I had handed him a dead rat and he dropped it on the blotter on his desk. It would be in the waste-paper basket before I left the building. 'I cannot think of any reason why she should get in touch with me.'

I waved goodbye and left him to check the vital statistics of the young things he was going to interview the next day.

As I came into the outer office, the pretty girl looked up and smiled again. 'Your business completed, Mr Hawke?'

'Not quite ... Miss ...?'

'Kendal, Eve Kendal.'

'Well, Eve, you worked with Pamela Palfrey, didn't you?'

She nodded in a guarded fashion.

'Look, I'm a private detective. I'm trying to find Pamela. Her parents are worried about her. I don't suppose you know where she is?

Eve shook her head.

'What was she like? Did you get on with her?'

'She was OK. She was pleasant and amenable but we weren't close friends, if that's what you mean. She romanticized a bit.'

'About the movies.'

'Oh yes. She was mad about the pictures.'

'Did you ever go with her?'

Eve shook her head.

'Did she ever talk to you about Samantha?'

'Who's she?'

'A girlfriend.'

'Never heard Pamela mention her, but I sometimes had difficulty shutting her up about her boyfriend.'

The back of my neck tingled. 'She had a boyfriend?'

'Yes. A good-looking guy. Serious stuff too.'

'You sure she wasn't romanticizing about him as well?'

'Oh, no. Why should she?'

I thought of that podgy face in the snaps Palfrey had given me. There was every reason for her to romanticize about having a good-looking boyfriend.

'Did you ever see him?'

'Yes. He came to pick her up from here one day. I must admit he was good-looking.'

The back of my neck tingled again. Something was wrong here. Handsome blokes don't go around with plain Janes unless it's for some ulterior motive.

'What do you know about this good-looking fellow?'

'Not much. He's an actor and his name is Sam and he's got gorgeous chest hairs.' Eve giggled, her hand fluttering to her mouth. 'Sorry, but Pammie was always going on about his chest hairs. I haven't seen them personally, of course.' She giggled again.

A boyfriend called Sam, eh? No doubt he had been conveniently converted to the opposite sex especially for the benefit of Pamela's parents. He had become the girlfriend Samantha that she talked about incessantly. There was more to this devious little lady than had first seemed apparent.

'Did he have a last name?'

'Pammy always referred to him as Sam.'

'Where did he act?'

'I think he was out of work most of the time, but Pamela reckoned he'd be a big star one day'.

'Up there on the silver screen?'

'I guess so.'

'Didn't you find it odd that this good-looking Sam was

knocking about with Pamela who, not to put too fine a point on it, was hardly a looker?'

'Are you kidding? Pammie was very glamorous. Nearly all the male clients used to give her the eye.'

I shook my head in puzzlement. I just didn't get it. I delved into my jacket pocket and retrieved one of the snapshots of Pamela kindly donated by her father and passed it over to Eve. 'We are talking about the same girl here?' I said.

Eve stared at the picture. At first her face registered surprise and then amusement. 'Is this some kind of joke?'

I shook my head. 'No joke. That's Pamela Palfrey isn't it?'

Eve grinned. 'Yes, it's Pamela, but I've never seen her looking like this before. It's as though she's dressed up in a fancy dress competition. She's not wearing make-up and her hair's a mess ... and those clothes.' Eve's hand fluttered to her mouth to stifle another giggle.

'Tell me more,' I said, fascinated by this strange turn of events.

Eve cast a wary glance at Leo Epstein's door. 'I can do better than that. I can show you a photo of Pam as she really looked.' So saying she went to her own desk and pulled out a buff folder. 'Pam left in a bit of a hurry and she didn't clear out her desk properly. She left some things behind – some make-up and this picture of herself. I've kept her stuff in case she came back for it.'

She handed me the picture. It was no ordinary snap. It was mounted on card with an ivory border and had obviously been taken in a plush photographic studio. The lighting and the background was subtle and enhanced the features of the subject. Staring back at me was a stunningly beautiful girl with dark lustrous hair, large alluring eyes and full lips darkened into a glossy cupid's bow. She did, indeed, look like a film star. She was the beautiful princess distantly related to the dull-looking frump in the sepia photograph. What a transformation.

'That's the Pamela I knew,' said Eve, gently relieving me of the photograph so that she could return it to the folder and then back to her desk.

I nodded and smiled, lost in thought for a moment. 'That's the Pamela I knew.' The phrase struck a chord with me. It certainly wasn't the Pamela her parents knew. The girl was living a double life. The case grew more interesting by the minute.

I looked across at Eve Kendal who was studying me intently. She hadn't the contrived glamour of the Pamela Palfrey as represented in her studio portrait; Eve's beauty was more natural, less intimidating. I liked her.

'Is that all?' she asked gently.

'Not quite. Tell me, Miss Kendal, do you have a boyfriend?'

She shook her head shyly. 'No, but what's that to do with anything?'

Now it was my turn to be shy. 'Well, nothing really... I just wondered if you would care to come out with me for a drink this evening.' I couldn't believe I'd said it. Pretty girls usually bring out the mute in me. On this occasion my mouth had engaged before I had chance to reject the idea.

She looked uncertain. I had seen the kind of frown that wrinkled her brow before. It was a precursor to a refusal.

'I assure you that I am fully house-trained,' I added, in a vain attempt to be jaunty. I made a mental note to myself: Don't try to be jaunty in future.

The frown faded. 'OK then. But could we go to the pictures? I'm dying to see the new Tiger Blake picture.'

Just in time I was able to prevent myself from blurting out that I had already seen it. 'That would be great,' I said with a smile. I didn't mind sitting through the movie again, not if I was in the presence of such a choice piece as Eve Kendal.

'It's on at the Astoria, near Leicester Square. What say we meet outside at seven?'

'Miss Kendal, you have a date.' I slapped on my trilby and left, waiting until I was on the staircase before I out-grinned the Cheshire cat.

*

The evening at the cinema did not go as planned. My reason for asking Eve for a date was two-fold. I was sure that I could learn more about Pamela Palfrey if I talked with Eve in a more relaxed and intimate atmosphere, but more importantly I fancied the girl like mad.

To my delight, when I arrived at the Astoria five minutes early, Eve was already there. She was wearing a little more make-up than she had in the office and she looked gorgeous. What such a looker was doing going out with a one-eyed oddity like me I couldn't fathom. I didn't want to fathom: I was just grateful.

We sat in the stalls and endured a cartoon and a Laurel and Hardy short before there was an interval. I didn't want to rush the Pamela Palfrey business so I asked Eve about herself. 'There's nothing much to tell,' she said easily. 'I live with my mother – my father left us many years back – and I work at Epstein's. That's it. I'm a fairly dull person really. Now what about you? It must be exciting being a detective.'

I didn't reply. At that moment my eye had been caught by something a dozen or so rows further down from where we were sitting. It was a little face staring back at me. Dark haunted eyes underneath an unruly comma of dark, tousled hair. I rose from my seat and leaned forward, peering into the amber gloom. Could I be mistaken? The face gazing at me blanched in recognition, the eyes widening in panic. No, I wasn't mistaken: it was my errant lodger. It was the boy, Peter.

Without a word to Eve, I jumped to my feet, rushed to the end of the row, squeezing past a number of irate patrons in the process. As I reached the aisle my feet became entangled with someone's shopping bag. I lost my balance and stumbled to my knees. Muttering an apology to the bag's owner, a fat woman in a fur coat with a face like a collapsed balloon, I leapt to my feet in time to see that Peter had also left his seat. He was nimbler than I and was already racing across the front of the cinema. I followed in his wake, cursing as I realized that the lights were dimming. As shapes turned into shadows, I spotted Peter slipping behind the velvet curtains by the illuminated Lavatories sign. I went after him and found myself in a draughty, dimly lighted corridor. Had he gone into the Gents hoping to hide in there? As I took hold of the door handle, I heard a loud crashing noise and, glancing further along the corridor, I saw that the emergency exit doors had been thrust wide open. I ran into the alleyway beyond the doors just in time to catch sight of Peter turning the corner at speed. By the time I reached the street I knew I had lost him. I gazed down the darkening thoroughfare where he had merged into a shifting mass of indistinct silhouettes. That was the second time I'd let him get away. I swore and hit my fist on the damp wall.

By the time I returned to the body of the cinema, the big picture had started. Allowing my eyes to get used to the strange flickering half-light, slowly I made my way back to the row where I had been sitting with Eve. How was I going explain my strange behaviour to her, I wondered. What sort of lunatic did she think I was? Someone who leaps from his chair without explanation or apparent reason and races around the cinema. Whatever she thought, the explanation would have to wait. When I reached the row, I could see quite clearly that she had gone. That's good going, Johnny, I thought. A double loser in one night. It must be some sort of record, even for you.

I left the Astoria just as Tiger Blake broke the bad news to the rest of the crew of the light aircraft: 'We're about to crash into uncharted jungle.'

eight

He had been at his club since the early evening. He had retreated there after a fraught meeting with his agent where he'd paced up and down the office, waving the letter about, cursing and calling into doubt the parentage of all the executives of Renown Pictures. His agent tried to calm him down but failed. He had no honest words of comfort to offer. It was bad news and this particular grey cloud had no silver lining.

He had intended to get drunk at his club, to blot out the reality of what had been his blackest day, but after the first brandy and soda failed to soften his anger, he grew more bitter. How could those bastards do it to him after all the money he had made for them? Twelve fucking films – all of which had made money, good money – and now he was being cast on the scrap heap. After he finished the picture he was working on, they weren't going to renew his contract. They were getting rid of him. What was the phrase they used: 'Our relationship has run its natural course.'

Bastards!

They were not only taking away his occupation, but his lifestyle and his importance. With one letter they had made him an ex-star – a has-been. Somehow he would get his own back. He wasn't finished yet. He'd show them. Somehow. This defiant resolution seemed to ease his pain and he ordered another drink.

'Hello there,' said one of the familiar faces in the club in passing. 'Saw the latest effort. Jolly good show.'

He nodded and smiled, acknowledging the compliment. There you are, he thought, after the man had passed by, 'Jolly good show'. And so it bloody was ... and yet. He took another gulp of brandy. What he really needed now was a woman. He could expel all his pent-up frustration, anger and energy in bedding a woman. Not the one at home, though. An anonymous red-blooded woman who would put a bit of passion into her lovemaking; someone who would do more than just lie there and wait patiently for the ghastly business to be over. That's what he needed. Someone uninhibited, experienced and available. And, by George, he knew where to find one – for a price, of course. But what the hell, why not end this ghastly day on a pleasurable note?

A telephone call would do it. But he wasn't going to use the club's facilities. They were far from private and the old bores who haunted the place were notorious for eavesdropping. He slipped out of the club to a nearby phone box. He was in luck – in this instance anyway. The lady was available, but not until later that evening. He could wait – the anticipation would be part of the pleasure.

After escaping from the man with the black eye patch, Peter roamed the streets aimlessly for an hour or so before he found himself outside a small fish and chip shop. The smell of the hot food lured him in and he spent some more of his precious money on cod and chips which the woman at the counter wrapped up in newspaper after he'd salted and vinegared them. He found an empty shop doorway some hundred yards away where he crouched and devoured his cooked supper in no time. After he had finished he felt warm and happy inside. He could have easily curled up in the doorway and fallen asleep, but after his experience of the previous night, he was wary of such places. He had to find somewhere more private, a spot where people didn't pass by. And he thought he knew where. Wiping his greasy hands down the sides of his raincoat, he set off with determination.

As he made his way through the darkened and deserted streets, he stopped at every litter bin and dustbin collecting any newspapers he could find. By the time he reached the perimeter of Regent's Park he reckoned he had enough to make a reasonable mattress for himself. If he could get into the park, he was sure he could find some cover, maybe even a shelter, where he could kip down for the night. He knew the gates would be closed, so he'd have to find a place where he could clamber over the railings. He didn't know what time it was but he knew it must be late. The moon was high and there wasn't a soul about. It was best he made his move now. Choosing a dark spot, shaded by an overhanging chestnut, he flung his cache of newspapers over the railings and was just about make his first assault on the metal barrier when he heard a strange cry some little distance away. It was like one of those ghostly moans he'd read about in ghost stories: long and very sad. It frightened him. And then he saw a solitary figure staggering along on the other side of the road from him. The moan came again, quieter this time, more like an agonized sob. Terrified, Peter pressed himself against the railings, deep into the shadows.

As the figure grew nearer, he saw that it was a man, moving slowly and sobbing. Suddenly he stopped, motionless for a moment, and then he made some attempt to pull himself together. Peter had never seen a grown-up so distressed, except Mrs Kitchen who lived two floors below. She went crazy when she learned that her son had been killed in a bomb blast, wailing and shrieking she was and tearing at her hair, but she was a woman and it was all right for women to cry – but not grown men.

As the boy watched in the shadows, the man gradually pulled himself together. He wiped his face with a handkerchief and, as he did so, Peter observed that his hands were stained with some dark shiny blotches. Then he pulled up the collar of his overcoat. In doing so, he lifted his head and his features could be seen clearly in the moonlight. Peter almost wet himself as he recognized the man.

It was Tiger Blake.

nine

As I opened the newspaper the following morning, after my abortive date with Eve, the first thing I saw was the face of Pamela Palfrey staring back at me. It wasn't the Pamela Palfrey as represented in the snapshots given to me by her father. This one was the glamorous version. But there was that same strange haunted look in the eyes, despite the fact that she was smiling. The picture was placed below the headline: BRUTAL KILLING.

Apparently Pammie Palmer, a model, had been found stabbed to death in the bedroom of her flat by her boyfriend Sam Fraser, late last night. He could think of no reason or motive for such 'a senseless killing'. Nevertheless he had been taken in for questioning and was 'helping the police with their enquiries'. I grimaced. I bet he was. There was no mention of the girl's parents, or of how she had become a Palmer, or how she had become a model.

I got on the phone straight away to Scotland Yard. Luckily I just caught David before he was about to leave the office on a job.

'What can I do for you this time?' he asked. His voice was weary and a little impatient.

'The girl that was found murdered last night ...'

'What about her?'

'I was trying to trace her. Her parents are clients of mine.'

'Were clients, don't you mean? Looks like it's case closed, eh, old son?'

'It's not as simple as that. The name you have is not her real one. There's something fishy about the whole business.'

'Really ...'

'It seems that she was living two lives.'

There was a pause, and I could almost hear the cogs of David's brain turning over on the crackly line. 'Look, Johnny,' he said at length, 'give me five minutes and I'll get back to you.'

When the phone rang again, it was a different voice on the other end – more polished and businesslike. 'Mr Hawke, this is Chief Inspector Alan Knight, a colleague of David Llewellyn. I'm handling the Pammie Palmer murder case, I believe you have information which may be of use to us....'

An hour later I was cradling a mug of hot sweet tea in New Scotland Yard, sitting across the desk from Detective Chief Inspector Alan Knight. He was a tall, broad-shouldered fellow with a face that seemed to have been chiselled out of granite. It was uniformly grey, full of gritty, sharp corners and the mouth looked as though it hadn't seen a smile in a long time. I had told him the story so far, including my belief that Pammie had been maintaining two lives for a while – the frumpy, dull girl who mooned over movie stars and the pretty model with the actor boyfriend.

'It was only recently that she had dumped the old persona to move on. She left her parents and it seems she went to live with Sam,' I said, lighting a cigarette. I offered the packet to Knight but he shook his head.

'Why did she do it?' he asked.

I shrugged. 'I don't know. I can guess maybe but that's nothing for you to go on.'

'Share your guess, Mr Hawke. The more ideas we have, the better I like it.'

I hated being called Mr Hawke, but I reckon Chief Inspector Knight would have had trouble getting his tongue around the familiarity of 'Johnny'. It struck me that he was the kind of fellow who had only just made first name terms with his wife.

'Having met the parents and heard their side of the story, it seems to me that Pamela became the daughter they wanted her to be, plain, dull and obedient. She put on a performance for them. That would have appealed to the actress in her. She dressed in frumpy, shapeless clothes which hid her figure and wore no make up. But away from home, she was what *she* wanted to be ...'

'A model ...' Knight added sarcastically.

'Maybe she needed her home base until she had secured enough money to fly the nest.'

'And so the caterpillar turned into a sexy butterfly and fluttered away.'

I winced. I hated mixed metaphors

'Something like that,' I said.

'So who killed her?'

'I have no idea.'

'No more guesses.'

'That gets dangerous. I'd need more evidence. Who do you think did it?'

Knight leaned over his desk. 'To tell you that, I'm going to have to shatter a few of your illusions, Mr Hawke. As you well know the term "model" has more than one interpretation. I don't know about our Pammie being a pretty butterfly, but it's fairly certain she was a prostitute and that her boyfriend Samuel Fraser was her pimp. Fraser already has a record for living off immoral earnings.'

I wasn't shocked. I half expected it. But I felt sad, sad for Pamela's parents but mostly sad for Pamela. The world of glamour and money reduced down to a sordid sexual trade.

'So Fraser is really in the spotlight?'

'Full beam. Unless some other worm crawls out of the woodwork, yes. You got any other ideas?'

I shook my head. 'I'd only just started the case. Would you mind telling me what you know – how it happened?'

Knight sighed and glanced at his wristwatch. My usefulness was over; he didn't really want to be wasting his time with me.

'I really would appreciate it, Chief Inspector,' I greased, in the most ingratiating manner I could muster.

'Briefly then,' the granite face snarled. 'According to Fraser he got back to the flat in the early hours – sometime between one and two and found Pammie on the bedroom floor. She was in her nightgown and had been stabbed several times through the heart. He says he blacked out at the sight and it wasn't until he came round again about an hour later that he rang for the police.'

'Where had he been before returning to the flat?'

'He claims he was at The Carlton Casino in Storr Street. We've got one of our men checking his alibi now. But that may not help him. He says he left at twelve-thirty – which he may well have done – but he didn't ring the police until three-fifteen, which gives him plenty of time to come home, murder the girl, feign a blackout and then call us. It's thin stuff.'

'Motive?'

'Oh, I'm sure one will present itself.'

'Could she have been killed by a client?'

'Outside chance, I'd say. According to Fraser, she wasn't due to "model" for anyone last night. There was no evidence of any visitors.'

Before I could respond, there was a discreet knock at the door and a uniformed constable entered. 'Sorry to interrupt sir, but the pathologist thought you ought to have this urgently.' He passed over a note to Knight and vanished as quickly as he had arrived. Knight studied the note, his slab of a face giving nothing away and then he looked over at me, his lips crumbling slightly into a dry grin.

'You were asking about motive. Well, I think we've got one. It seems our little Pammie was with child.'

I saw the way that Knight's mind was working. There's not much money to be made out of a pregnant whore, so you kill her. It was simplistic, a theory built on very shaky foundations, but one that was likely to stop the police from looking any further and eventually lead to Samuel Fraser's conviction. Case closed and another feather in Chief Inspector Knight's cap. Maybe Fraser had done the dirty deed but, for the moment, I was prepared to give him the benefit of the doubt. If he had planned to murder the girl surely he could have come up with a better alibi than the one he'd given.

'I'd like to see Fraser if I might, Chief Inspector. It will help me tie up a few loose ends to my case.'

Knight sat back, his cold eyes glittering. 'Don't believe that would be a good idea, Mr Hawke. I thank you for your information but I think it would be better for both of us if you go now.'

I shrugged nonchalantly and rose, pushing my chair back. 'Have it your own way. I'll leave you to find out about the dark lady yourself.'

Knight's brow shifted into a frown. 'Dark lady? What dark lady? What are you on about?'

I grinned and touched my nose with my right forefinger. 'You'll no doubt find out.'

'Hawke, if you're withholding evidence—'

I'd lost the Mr now. 'Oh, I really doubt if it is at all relevant, but then again it could be very useful. It's not evidence as such, Chief Inspector ... just a piece of illuminating information. Educational, I'd say.'

Knight was angry now. He, too, rose from his chair, his body taut and his eyes registering anger. 'Look here!' he roared.

'No, Chief Inspector, you look here ... give me twenty minutes with Fraser and in return for your gracious favour I'll tell you all about the dark lady.'

For a moment I thought he was going to hit me. His massive hands clenched and shook but thankfully he fought manfully with his temper. After all it wouldn't do to hit a law-abiding citizen who was assisting the police in their investigation.

'Twenty minutes, eh? It can't hurt,' I added with a smile.

'I'll time you. And no word about the girl's pregnancy.'

I held up my hands in shock. 'I know better than that.'

Samuel Fraser was a good-looking fellow with dark curly locks which could have appeared as effeminate were it not for his sturdy features and a thin Errol Flynn-type moustache which adorned his upper lip. He stood up as I entered and I observed that he was quite short and stocky and therefore would never make it as a leading man.

I introduced myself as John Hawke, a detective on the case, and then offered him a cigarette. He took one and examined it closely. It was clear that he was used to a more superior brand than the lowly Craven A. However, this did not prevent him from lighting up and blowing the smoke in my direction.

'You are an actor?' I said.

His eyes brightened at this. 'Yes, I am an actor,' he replied in an actor's voice, dark, silky and slightly preposterous.

'Would I have seen you in anything?'

This stumped him momentarily. 'I was in a thing at the Albery last year and I had a part in the last Tiger Blake movie.'

'Ah, I've seen that,' I said, blowing my smoke back at him. Thirty love.

'What part did you play?'

'I was one of the Nazi radio operators ... a small role.'

I nodded as though in sympathy. 'A very small role.'

'They promised me a bigger part in the next one.'

'Let's hope you'll be able to take it.'

Fraser stopped mid-inhale as he realized the gravity of my observation. 'Look,' he said suddenly, stubbing out the half-smoked cigarette ferociously, 'this is a crazy notion. I didn't kill Pammie. She was my girl ... we were going to get married as soon—'

'As soon as she'd made enough money – lying on her back and thinking of England.'

'Why you ...!' He jumped up and took at swing at me. He missed by a mile and I laughed. He swung his fist again. This time I caught it in my hand and wrenched it sideways, bringing it down with some force on to the bench. Fraser gave a cry of pain and slumped back in his chair. Not only was he a little runt, but he was a cowardly one as well.

'Look, perhaps you don't realize how deep in the shit you are, but I'm here to tell you that unless you play straight, your next performance may well be on the gallows.'

This was something that the angry little fellow had not contemplated. The colour drained from his face and, as if by magic, beads of sweat appeared on his forehead.

'I didn't kill her. Honest. I didn't kill her. I really cared for her.'

Strangely enough, I believed him. This wasn't a performance any more. The voice had lost its cheap artifice.

'Any idea who did?'

He shook his head.

'Right, listen to me, Samuel, my boy, the police have got it into their thick heads that you're the chump who murdered Pammie. And indeed why should they look any further?'

'But you told me you're the police,' he said in a strange whining fashion.

I shook my head. 'I said I was a detective working on the case. I'm a private investigator. I was employed by Pammie's parents to find her. Or to be more precise to find Pamela Palfrey. You knew of your girlfriend's double life, of course.'

Fraser nodded. 'She was Pamela when I first met her. It was me who suggested she change her name.'

'Well, under whatever name we use, I've found the Palfreys' daughter for them, after a fashion. Now I reckon it's my duty to find her murderer as well. And that's how I can help you.'

'Help me ...?'

'Strange as it may seem, I don't reckon you did kill her. Don't ask me why; I just have an instinct about these things. And, anyway, it seems sensible and a matter of principle to take the opposite view to Detective Chief Inspector Knight. But before I can be of assistance to you, you've got to do your bit.'

'What do you mean?'

'Tell me all about Pammie. How you met and how she ended up being ... your girl. The whole story and the truth.'

'Can I have another fag?'

'As long as you smoke this one.'

He nodded.

I passed over the packet. 'OK, Sammy, now spill the beans.'

ten

Sammy's Story

I first saw Pamela, as she was then, at the Regent dance hall. It was about six months ago. I was on the prowl that night. I needed another girl. My acting work had dried up again and I was desperately short of money. With a girl, the right girl, I could easily make fifty quid a week. As soon as I saw her, I knew she was the one. She was special: she had star quality.

I got talking to her in the bar. Bought her a drink. Spun her a tale about my illustrious acting career and by the end of the evening we were smooching under the mirrorball. At the time I thought I was doing all the leading but looking back on it, I can see that I was the one being led. I was aware I couldn't rush it with Pamela. She was not like the other girls I'd been involved with. But I didn't need to force the pace. The whole thing took off quickly.

We did the traditional thing for a while. Saw each other on dates: trips to the cinema, walks in the park, dancing, meals out. All that stuff. But we both knew we were marking time. We were holding the passion back, just to go through the hoops. Once we became lovers, the whole thing became so simple.

She was desperate to leave home and live the film-star life and she came with a secret nest egg. She'd been saving for years, squirrelling away various amounts, until she had quite a sum. Enough for us to start renting a flat near Regent's Park.

Don't get me wrong. The money wasn't that important. I really cared for her. I loved her. And I believe she loved me. But we were both practical sorts as well. Nothing wrong with that.

It was me who persuaded her to change her name to Pammie Palmer, partly to cut herself off from her past life really and to stop her parents turning up and trying to drag her back. She like the idea. She loved playing the part and she played it up to the hilt. And so she became Pammie Palmer.

Once we moved in to our flat, I came clean about my less than glowing prospects and wondered if she would agree to entertaining a few gentlemen a couple of nights a week to help pay for the groceries. I knew I was taking a risk, but things were desperate. I really expected her to throw something at me and storm out; instead she smiled and said yes. Just like that. No hesitation. She thought the idea was exciting, dramatic – straight out of a film, I guess. She didn't see it as sordid in any way. Apparently, she had done it before for money and saw nothing immoral in the transaction. That's how she'd helped to build up her nest egg. I'd been the naïve one all along.

I'd been doing some extra work down at Denham. Walk ons. A man in a crowd. That sort of thing. Anyway there were a few fellows down there who knew me and my services. I was soon able to get enough clients for Pammie to be busy two or three nights a week. As a business venture it was very successful, but there was a complication. I began to fall in love with her. She was very beautiful, but it wasn't just that. She had a way with her that was so endearing, so thoroughly captivating. I couldn't help myself. And, of course, I grew jealous. I didn't like the idea of other men touching her. But, apparently, she did. She liked the danger, the excitement, the glamour of it. She often referred to it as 'my performance'.

Then one night, a 'client' stayed longer than arranged. He'd drunk too much champagne and passed out and I came back to find him half dressed, lying on the bedroom floor. Pammie thought that it was hilarious but I was beside myself with anger. I hated myself for setting up the whole wretched business and for falling in love with her and I hated her for enjoying it so much.

I threw the fellow out and then begged her to put a stop to

it. By accident I had witnessed the reality of the situation. I suppose I must have blanked it from my mind what Pammie was really up to when she 'entertained' a client. But now ... I'd had my nose rubbed in it.

I said it must stop. I promised to find the money somehow, even if it meant getting an ordinary job. 'How will you earn enough to pay for this?' she jeered, throwing her arms wide as though embracing the flat.

It was then that I asked her to marry me.

She hadn't expected that and it stopped her in her tracks. It wasn't part of the script, you see. She didn't know whether to laugh or cry. After a moment she ran to my arms and as we kissed, I don't think I was ever as happy in my whole life. As for her ... I reckon it was just another fulfilling dramatic moment.

We made love that night and it was real and special. I thought it bonded us together for life. An act of genuine passion which was stronger than any marriage certificate or wedding ring. The next morning Pammie agreed not to see any more men. I can't tell you how happy this made me.

In the days that followed I made an extra effort of going round all the agents scrounging for work and by night I went to the casino in a desperate attempt to win some money to keep our flat on. My modest wins helped, but I knew our finances were slipping. I prayed I'd get a good acting job that paid well. But nothing happened.

Then, after a time, I suspected Pammie was seeing clients again. She didn't need me to set the meetings up anymore. There were enough men out there who had her number. I knew there was nothing I could do about it. If I challenged her and it was true – as I had no doubt it was – we'd be finished, washed up. And I couldn't face that.

I was at the end of my tether. You see I never expected all this – love, involvement, commitment. They were not on my agenda. These feelings were not only foreign to me before I met Pammie, but I had despised them as weak and pathetic emotions in others. From the start I had thought of myself as the puppet master pulling her strings, but I was wrong: she had been in control all the time. To the very end.

The night she died, I'd been to the casino. I was desperate to come out with a big win. As the night wore one, I lost more and more. I drank heavily, too, to cushion myself from the pain of failure, I guess. When my wallet was empty, I left. The cold air and the full realization of what I'd done, blown my last £200, soon sobered me up. By the time I got back to the flat, I was ready for the showdown. I was never to have it.

The door of the flat was unlocked and the lights in all the rooms were blazing. When I went into the bedroom … well, what I saw was Pammie lying on her back on the bed. She was in her negligée and there was blood seeping on to the eiderdown from her chest. Her eyes were open and so was her mouth as though she was crying out for help. Silently crying for help.

That's what I saw, but I couldn't believe my eyes. I just couldn't believe that it was real. It must be some awful mirage or something. I sat on the edge of the bed gazing down at her for what seemed ages. I suppose I was waiting for her to wake up. Or start laughing, saying that she had been pretending to give me a shock. It wasn't blood really, it was tomato ketchup.

But she didn't. She just kept on staring at me with those dark, sightless eyes. And then I leaned forward and touched her cheek. She was already cold. I could feel the deadness of her skin. I began to shiver all over and some noise in my head thundered, blotting out everything else. It was then I must have blacked out for the next thing I knew, I was lying on the bed staring at the ceiling. For a moment, I forgot where I was. You know, that few seconds of amnesia when you first wake up. And then I remembered. It came back to me in all its awfulness. I squeezed my eyes shut, hoping and praying that it had all been some kind of crazy dream. But Pammie was still there, her eyes still staring at me and the blood still seeping on to the sheets.

That's when I rang the police.

I'm no angel and I've done some things I'm not particularly proud of, but I didn't kill Pammie. I couldn't kill her: I loved her too much.

You've got to believe me.

eleven

When he'd finished, Samuel Fraser turned his head away from me so that I wouldn't see him crying. It wasn't an act; he was genuinely cut up. I felt sorry for the poor devil. I sat quietly for some time turning his story over and over in my head while playing with my tab end in the metal ashtray, pushing all the feathery ash into one little heap. It was a soothing process. Certainly the picture of Pammie Palmer was one that was vastly removed from the one presented by her parents – the dull, dumpy little girl who mooned over film stars – but somehow it all rang true. Pammie was a performer, a frustrated actress who turned her life into a dramatic movie. Unfortunately the climax had been tragic. In a strange way, she would have probably relished the notoriety and high drama of her final curtain call.

'If it wasn't you, Mr Fraser, who killed Pammie,' I said at length, 'then it must have been her last client, whoever he was. The man she had been with that night, the secret punter.'

'Yeah, I suppose so,' he said reluctantly, brushing the moisture from his cheek. He still didn't want to believe that Pammie had been two-timing him behind his back, even if it had been purely a matter of business.

I passed over my pack of cigarettes. If ever a man was in need of nicotine, I reckon he was. 'So,' I said briskly, 'you'll have names.'

'Names?'

'Of her clients.'

'Oh, I couldn't ...'

'Oh, but you could and you will.'

'But it's more than my life's worth to give away—'

'Let's face it, Sammy, *your* life isn't worth the price of a Woolworth's comb at present,' I snapped. 'If you don't help me, you'll be measured for a rope collar before you can say good-night sweetheart. I need names.'

He ran his fingers through his hair. 'I ... I don't know them all. Pammie ... Pammie had her own. It started with a few guys at Denham.'

'Names, Sammy, names.'

For the second time he stubbed out a half-smoked cigarette with at least five minutes more pleasure in it. I winced at the waste. 'You got a paper and pencil?' he said.

I passed over my notepad and trusty HB. Sammy scribbled down four names on the pad and passed it back to me.

'Those are the only ones I know, but I can't think that any of them could murder—'

'Classic mistake. We're all capable of murder in certain circumstances.'

'You'll help me, then.'

I slipped the pad into my inside pocket.

'I'll find Pammie's killer, if that's what you mean.'

As I left the cell, Detective Chief Inspector Knight was waiting for me in the corridor outside. He was looking at his watch. 'That was half an hour,' he sneered, in an accusatory tone.

'Doesn't time fly when you're having fun,' I responded with a smile.

'I hope you got what you wanted.'

'For what it's worth, Chief Inspector, I'm fairly sure that Samuel Fraser did not kill the girl.'

'Oh, and what makes you so sure?'

'I just believe him.'

'Hah!' Knight virtually spat out the exclamation. 'We're a little more practical at Scotland Yard. If we believed every villain who claimed he was innocent, we'd never make an arrest.'

I nodded indulgently and turned to leave, but old granite features grabbed my arm. It was as though it had been placed in a metal vice. 'Before you go, I need to know about the dark lady. Remember.'

I gazed at him blankly for a moment and then with a shy grin I feigned recall. 'Oh, yes, of course; the dark lady. Her name is Beulah White, a fine jazz singer. She does two sets at The Velvet Cage on Dean Street each evening. You should drop in some time and catch her. She's good.'

'And what has she to do with this case?'

'Why nothing at all. I just thought you'd like to know about her. After a day arresting people, her voice could help you unwind.' I slipped on my hat, quickly extricated myself from Knight's loosened grasp and nipped up the stairs before his temper ignited.

'Hawke!' he yelled angrily, as I reached the top, his voice reverberating all the way up the stairs. Without a pause I passed through the door, thus blocking off the stream of abuse which no doubt was issuing from the sturdy mouth of Detective Chief Inspector Knight.

It was late morning when Constable Arthur Dobson made the discovery. He had been on duty in Baker Street and things had been very quiet. Obviously, all the spivs and the low life were keeping out of his way. They knew not to be careless when Arthur Dobson was around. Keen as mustard he was, even if he said so himself. On a whim, he decided to have a stroll through Regent's Park to see if there was anything there to interest him. Perhaps he could nab a vagrant for sleeping rough in one of His Majesty's parks. That would suit him. An easy bit of business and another notch on his record. Unfortunately for him he found the park as quiet as the streets. It was becoming increasingly clear that he would have to return to the station empty-handed on this occasion. The desk sergeant will be disappointed, he told himself. Little did he know that the desk sergeant couldn't give a damn.

As compensation for his arid morning, Constable Dobson decided to have a crafty fag to cheer himself up. Looking around to check that there was no one about, he slipped into the shrubbery and took a cigarette and matches from his coat pocket. Slipping the cigarette into his mouth, he lit up. As the match flared in the gloom, he saw something on the ground about a yard away from where he was standing, something that caused him to start and the cigarette dropped silently from his open mouth.

He knelt by the object and lit another match. There was no doubt that it was a body. Curled up in a foetal position it was the body of a young boy.

The Palfrey household was just how I imagined it. A solid, middle-class, red-roofed house in a solid, middle-class area of Pinner with a tidy lawn, perky little anonymous blooms in the weed-free borders and pristine net curtains billowing at the windows. I was not relishing the visit but I felt it was my duty to pass on the bad tidings. After all they were my clients and I reckoned that my job wasn't over yet, not until I'd nailed their daughter's killer. I hoped that I'd got there ahead of the police because I knew from past experience that they could be rather ham-fisted in the condolence stakes. Anyway I supposed that informing parents of the death of their daughter was very low in the priorities of Chief Inspector Knight. He had other things on his mind like charging Samuel Fraser. It wouldn't have surprised me if he had forgotten all about the murdered girl's parents in his zeal to obtain a conviction.

I felt sure that the Palfreys wouldn't have tied in the fuzzy picture of Pammie Palmer which was in the papers that morning with their beloved plain-Jane daughter. At least I hoped so.

My stomach churned unpleasantly as I rang the door bell. Some instinct told me it would play a tune. It would not be a simple bring-bring, but in keeping with the nicety of the neighbourhood, there would be a tune. And there was. I heard good old 'Greensleeves' reverberating down the hallway.

After a time, Freda Palfrey answered the door. She seemed smaller and paler than I remembered her from the day before. Dark shadows formed grey semi-circles under her vacant eyes. Of course, I told myself, she had put on a brave made-up face to come to town. Lipstick, powder and the other tools of feminine artifice had been brought into play to deceive the world, to hide the pain and anguish of a distressed mother. In the home, such deceit was not necessary. And now, here I was, about to put a final seal on that distress. I hated myself.

'Mr Hawke … we weren't expecting you. Do you have news?'

My face must have told her all.

She stared for a moment at me with a mixture of disbelief and horror. I had come with the tidings that she feared the most, but those which in the deepest secret hidey-hole of her heart she knew would come to her eventually. Her little girl was dead.

'I'm sorry,' I said quietly. Inadequate though it was, I didn't know what else to say.

Her eyes moistened and her lip trembled but she held herself erect and fought against her rising emotions. 'You'd better come in and tell us all about it.'

She led me into a spick and span parlour and left me there while she went to find her husband. 'He'll be in the garden shed,' she muttered matter-of-factly.

There were two pictures of Pamela in the room but they were of the Pamela of old: plain, dumpy and submissive. She gazed at me unwaveringly with docile, simpering eyes. Ever the actress was our Pamela. There was also a sepia-tinted print on a side table of Mr and Mrs Palfrey on their wedding day. He was wearing a tight pinstripe suit which looked as though it had been painted on while she was in a very frilly wedding dress with a mob cap of a matching material on her head. They looked happy and normal. He had a bright face and a jaunty moustache and his features suggested nothing of the pedantic, small-minded dullard he was to become. She, on the other hand, while pretty seemed frail and grateful.

'Mr Hawke.'

I turned to face the same couple standing side by side on the threshold of the room as though they were waiting for my permission to enter. What decay thirty years had wrought upon them. They had become other people and somehow the joy of living had leaked out of them.

I nodded, not trusting myself with words just yet. Taking on the role of host, with a gesture I bid them sit down. Clasping each other's hands, they perched on the faded moquette sofa.

'What is it then?' asked Mr Palfrey, already guessing the gist of my response.

'I'm sorry to tell you that ... your daughter ... Pamela ... is dead.'

I got no further. Mrs Palfrey clamped her hand to her mouth and gave searing moan before melting sideways into the arms of her husband.

'She was murdered,' I added.

'Murdered!' Palfrey reacted with anger. 'By whom, for God's sake!'

'That has yet to be discovered, but the police are interviewing her ... boyfriend.' I used this rather circumspect expression because I didn't think this couple were quite ready for the idea that their beloved daughter had a lover.

'Boyfriend. She had a boyfriend! Was it he who lured her away from us, from her home?' Palfrey had shaken off his wife now and was staring at me as though I was responsible for his daughter's death.

I shook my head. 'I'm afraid the story I have to tell will distress you. But it's the truth and I suppose it has to be faced.'

'Don't talk in riddles, man. What are you trying to say?'

'Pamela deceived you. At home she was the demure rather plain little girl you wanted her to be, but it was a part she played according to your expectations. In reality she was a pretty girl, glamorous even, with an appetite for life and she was determined to enjoy it. She was just waiting for the opportunity to shed her old life with you and step into a new and exciting one in the bright lights of London. The cinema was her drug; it showed her there was another world out there.'

'A wild and wicked one,' asserted Palfrey, but now his manner was more subdued.

'That was part of the attraction. She met an out-of-work actor and formed a relationship with him. Then she left here to go and live with him.'

'Live with him! In sin?'

'If you mean without marrying him, yes.'

'I ... just cannot believe this. It's some nasty fairy tale.'

Mrs Palfrey sat up and wiped her eyes. 'No, it's not, Donald. Mr Hawke wouldn't be that cruel. What he's telling us is the truth. You know it. I know it. We both sensed ... we both ... but we never spoke.'

For a long moment there was an awful silence while both parents tried to readjust to the reality of the situation. Their little girl was dead and no amount of grief, regret, recriminations, anger or money was going to bring her back.

It was Mrs Palfrey who spoke first, her eyes moist but calm and her voice even and under control. It was then that I saw that in fact she was much the stronger of the two. The husband was all bluster and routine – his way of keeping the truth at bay. She, on the other hand, had a firmer grasp on reality. Her stern features and flinty eyes suggested to me that she believed unpleasant facts were something to accept and deal with, not to deny or ignore.

'Can you tell us the whole story, please? How she came to be murdered ... and everything.'

I nodded. 'D'you mind if I smoke?'

For a fraction of a second, Palfrey's posture stiffened as though he was going to refuse, but it was an automatic reaction and the moment passed. I told them all I knew about Pamela, her relationship with Samuel Fraser and the manner of her death. As I unveiled this horror tale, the silent Palfreys sat before me, melting into each other like two wax effigies caught in a heat-wave. Their faces were drained of expression and emotion. I was the storyteller from their worst nightmares.

When I had finished they still maintained the melted tableau for a long while before Mr Palfrey broke away, strode angrily to the window and gazed sightlessly through the net curtains at the prim garden beyond. 'Are you seriously asking us to believe that our Pamela, our daughter, slept with men for money? That she was a whore?' He roared the words at the window.

At this outburst, Mrs Palfrey gave a low moan.

'It isn't something I would tell you if it wasn't absolutely certain it was true.'

'She was ... a whore?'

I couldn't respond to that one without twisting the knife further.

'It was her choice, Father,' said Mrs Palfrey. 'Perhaps we ... protected her too much. Stifled her.'

'We were loving parents ... and she does this to us.'

'I know all this is a terrible shock to you, but we must not lose sight of the most important thing now, which is to catch her murderer.'

'Well. The police have done that. This so-called boyfriend. Her pimp.'

I shook my head. 'I am convinced that he didn't do it. He loved her.'

'Loved her!' snarled Palfrey. 'But he let her sleep with other men. What kind of monster is that?'

'We don't all share the same moral outlook and he did try to make her stop when he realized how much he cared for her.'

Palfrey turned to face me, his body shaking and his face twisted with conflicting emotions of anger, pain and disbelief. 'I don't understand the world any more. I just....' He sat on the arm of the sofa shaking his head.

'Can we see her?' asked his wife softly. 'I'd like to see her?'

'The police will be along shortly. I am sure and they can arrange all that. I just felt I had to come and tell you myself.'

'That was very thoughtful of you, Mr Hawke.' Her eyes were moist and sad.

'As I said, I am still on the case. If the police convince themselves that Fraser is the guilty party, they'll shut down the
investigation. They'll not bother to look elsewhere. If that
happens the real killer will get away.'

'Are you certain this pimp fellow is innocent?' Palfrey said,
looking me squarely in the face.

'I am.'

'You have evidence?'

I shook my head. 'Not yet, but....'

He turned his back on me and stared out of the window once
more.

'Then you must go on, Mr Hawke,' he said, at length, his
voice cracking with emotion. 'Complete your investigations ...
for us.'

For the first time, I felt sorry for this little man. He was adrift
in an open boat floating on alien waters.

'I will,' I said simply.

Without turning round, he said, 'Freda, the money.'

'Yes, dear,' she replied, and opened a drawer in the sideboard
extracting the large envelope of cash that she had brought to
my office. She held out a wad of notes.

I shook my head. 'I don't want your money now, Mrs
Palfrey. We can think about fees when the job is done.'

Awkwardly I rose to leave. 'I'll see myself out. I'll be in
touch.'

Before either of them had chance to respond I was out of the
room heading for the front door. At that moment I wanted to
put as much distance between me and the Palfreys as possible.
The pain of their ruined lives was unbearable. Nothing I could
do, even catching Pamela's killer, could repair the damage. A
darkness had fallen upon them which could never be lifted. It
was good to get out into the fresh air once again.

twelve

Lunchtime found me nursing a pint in The Guardsman and
studying the names on Fraser's list: the intimates of Miss
Pamela Palfrey – deceased. Of the four names, two were
completely unknown to me, one rang a very faint bell down
a long dark corridor but one name was definitely very
familiar. Because of this, that particular fellow went to the
top of the list. I was just pondering how exactly I was going
to deal with the matter in practical terms, when I felt a hand
on my shoulder; it was a hand well accustomed to feeling
collars.

'I suspected you'd be in here,' said Inspector David Llewellyn
as he plonked down beside me, his pint glass accidentally
clinking against mine. 'Cheers, man.'

'Cheers,' I replied, managing a half-smile.

'Oh, it's Mr Gloomy Pants is it? I thought it would be all
grins and winks after you got one over on old Dirty Knight this
morning. Mind you, from what I've heard, you'd better keep
out of his way in near future. He's gunning for you.'

'You know, I reckon he's the kind of chap I'd prefer as an
enemy rather than a friend.'

David chuckled. 'I'd say his missus feels the same way.
Anyway, I'm not here for idle chatter. I have some news for you.
I think your boy's turned up.'

'Peter?'

'Don't know his name yet. About eleven, dark-haired, blue
gabardine mac.'

I nodded. 'Where is he?'

'Charing Cross Hospital. One of the lads on the beat discovered him curled up in bushes somewhere in Regent's Park. He was unconscious when he was found. He's feverish and running a high temperature but they reckon he'll be all right.'

'Can I see him?'

David raised an eyebrow. 'We're getting paternal all of a sudden, aren't we?'

'Come off it, a lad from the valleys doesn't know what paternal means.'

'I've been reading to improve myself.'

'Well, it's not working.'

We grinned together, enjoying the brief moment of jokey camaraderie.

'So,' I said at length, with mock impatience, 'can I see him?'

David glanced at his watch. 'OK, but we'd better be quick, I've got a briefing in an hour.'

'So what are we waiting for,' I asked, standing up and draining my pint.

Charing Cross Hospital is a great Victorian mausoleum of a place, all cracked white tiles and pungent with the acrid smell of disinfectant. It had the architectural finesse of a medieval madhouse. One felt, traversing its labyrinthine and featureless corridors, that you would never find your way out again. You were doomed for ever to haunt these winding white pathways, occasionally encountering other lost souls who had met the same fate. This sense of imprisonment was increased by the windows, what few there were, being taped in a criss-cross fashion as precaution against air raids. It was difficult to believe that there was a vibrant, living, breathing city bustling away beyond those thick foreboding walls.

The patient we had come to see was in a side room of the children's ward. A burly porter in a shiny blue uniform stood on guard outside the door. David showed him his credentials and with a silent nod of the head, the sentry allowed us into the room. A small window threw a grey shaft of light on to the bed, illuminating the gaunt face of a young boy asleep, his small body apparently lost under a mound of sheets and blankets. His skin was shiny clean and tinged pink with fever.

It was Peter.

'Is this the boy?' asked David, his voice muted to match the atmosphere of the sick room.

'Yes, it's him. He looks terrible.'

'You'll see far worse in here, I can tell you that.' The voice came from behind us. We turned to see a thin-faced, dark-haired sister. She looked careworn and tired, but there was a businesslike brightness about her eyes which was comforting.

'Which one of you is the policeman?' she asked matter-of-factly.

David raised his hand.

'And are you the father?'

I shook my head. 'No.'

'A relative?'

I shook my head again. 'I found the boy sheltering in a doorway a few nights ago and gave him a bed for the night. But he ran away.'

'The poor mite. Well, you'll get no sense out of him today, I can tell you that. He's got a high fever and we'll have to wait for Nature to take her course on that before he'll be *compos mentis*.'

I leant over Peter and laid my hand on his forehead. It was hot and damp. The coolness of my hand caused him to stir briefly, his face grimacing as though some dark memory had returned to trouble his dreams.

'It's best to leave him be for the moment. He's in good hands here. He'll pull through. Young 'uns do if there's a glimmer of a chance. They have so much to live for.'

The speech was a preamble to her ushering us out of the room.

'May I visit him again?' I asked.

'I don't see why not ... if the police say it's all right.'

'No problem there, Sister,' said David, edging towards the door. 'I reckon at the moment old Johnny here is the only real friend he's got.'

*

It was good to get out into the fresh air again and to be assailed by the hustle and bustle of the Strand. The real living world, however sad and dreary, was getting on with its own mundane business. Normality, what a precious state. I paused, lit a cigarette and inhaled deeply.

'This lad has really got to you, hasn't he?' observed David.

I said nothing. I couldn't think of anything to say. I really didn't understand my own feelings so I couldn't elaborate on them.

David sensed my dilemma and quickly checking his watch bade me farewell. 'Got that briefing. See you later.'

'Thanks,' I said as he left.

'Any time,' he called back, as he disappeared into the seething crowd of grey-faced pedestrians.

Well, my old son, I said to myself after a few moments, what next? Oh, yes, time to make an appointment with a film star.

I got back to the office around three o'clock. I had taken a fairly convoluted route to walk back partly because I wanted to play around with the odd jigsaw pieces of the Pamela Palfrey case in my mind to see if I could, without too much force, slip them together, interlock them, to see if I was anywhere near creating a picture or even sections of one. I wasn't. The little curves and sharp edges refused to bond. I needed more. The other reason for delaying my return was that I didn't fancy going back to my empty, grey, dusty office and the shabby room beyond knowing that they would only emphasize my own empty, grey, dusty and shabby life.

Once I'd closed the door, I poured myself a whisky and put a lively Benny Goodman record on the old wind-up gramophone hoping they would shake me out of the gloomy mood I was in. They helped a little and then I set to work.

I told the operator to put me through to Denham Studios. Once I'd connected to the switchboard – a lady sounding like she had a peg clamped to the end of her nose – I asked to speak to the public relations department of Regal Films. There was a long wait and then a voice of epicene qualities spoke shrilly down the line to me. 'Hello Regal, Tristan speaking.'

Resisting the urge to ask him how Isolde was these days, I went into my spiel. 'Hi there, this is Gus Andrews, y'know Gus Andrews of *ScreenTime*, the magazine of the stars. Well, we're doing a spread about handsome British heroes of the screen in the next issue and of course Gordon Moore, your very own Tiger Blake, is at the very top of our list. The pinnacle. I'm ringing to arrange an interview with Gordon so we can get the very latest on the new Tiger Blake.'

I hadn't gushed as much since I had a bad attack of diarrhoea on a holiday in Wales before the war.

Tristan seemed overwhelmed by my torrent and held back from replying for several seconds. '*ScreenTime*...? I don't think I know that one.'

'Oh we're quite new but we're catching up on the old-timers. By next year we'll be outselling *Picturegoer*.'

'Really! And that's so-o good.'

'We aim to be better ... with your help, Tristan.'

'My help?'

'The interview with Gordon ...?'

'Oh, yes. Well Mr Moore has just started filming the new Tiger Blake movie this week and he is ever so busy.'

'Surely you can squeeze me in. Publicity always helps a picture doesn't it?'

'Well, yes, that's what I'm here for.'

'Excellent. So when I can I come?'

'Just a minute, Mr ... er?'

'Gus Andrews: just call me Gus.'

'Oh, all right then, Gus. Just wait a minute while I check his shooting schedule.'

I waited while Tristan shuffled some sheets of paper, muttered to himself and sang a snatch of some song unfamiliar to me.

Eventually he came back to the telephone.

'Well, Gus, you're in luck. They've got a staggered shoot tomorrow. Mr Moore will be here late morning and then there's a break before a second session around five o'clock. I could try and arrange half an hour with him around three, if he's agreeable.'

'Oh, Tristan, that would be just dandy. I knew straight away that you were a man who could organize things.'

There was a pause and I sensed a chest being puffed out. 'We try our best. If you turn up at reception tomorrow around two-thirty and ask them to contact me in the Regal office, I'll come down and take you on to the set.'

'Excellent. I look forward to it.'

'So it's Mr Gus Andrews of *ScreenTime*, yes?'

'Certainly is.'

'Good, well I'll do all I can to make sure Mr Moore is agreeable.'

'Thank you, Tristan.'

'My pleasure ... Gus.'

'See you tomorrow.'

And so we parted company. I grinned. That was fun and the mission had been successful. After a while, I pulled out the paper that Sam Fraser had given me with the names of Pammie's clients and I put a tick by the name of Gordon Moore.

A couple more whiskies and several jolly jazz 78s later and I felt sufficiently brave to make my next phone call. This was one I was not looking forward to making. My fingers hovered over the receiver for some moments before I summoned up the nerve to start dialling. I got through without any trouble.

'Leo Epstein, solicitors. Can I help you?'

'Eve,' I said. Just one word but she recognized my voice straight away.

'Oh, it's you.' Hitler might have received a warmer response.

'I'm ringing to apologize for last night.'

'You needn't have bothered. From my point of view last night didn't happen ... and neither did you.'

I feared she was on the verge of putting the phone down. I had to rush on quickly.

'Please, please Eve ... Miss Kendal ... give me a chance to explain. I know it looks bad....'

'Bad? It looks like crazy to me. It seems you should be seeing a doctor or something. To go on a date with someone and then leave them to race round the cinema like a mad thing.'

'I was chasing someone. A runaway boy.' As I said these words I realized how pathetic and unconvincing they were. I had to over-egg this particular frail soufflé pretty quickly or she'd slam the receiver down on me. 'He's a boy involved in a murder case and in great danger. He's run away and was hiding in the cinema. When I saw him, I just had to try and catch him. It was a young life at risk.'

I was pleased with that last one: '... a young life at risk.' Surely that would break down the barrier. But Eve was not as easy a nut to crack as Tristan at Regal Films.

'You could have said something,' she replied, more petulant than angry now. 'You could have let me know what you were doing charging off like a bull elephant down the row. You know you stamped on one woman's corns and she complained to the usherette and I got such looks.'

I smiled at the thought. 'I'm truly sorry,' I said. 'I'll go away and shoot myself now and never bother you again. What more can I say?'

There was a hissing pause down the line and then: 'Well, I suppose you could say ... how about another date when I could really make amends for my strange behaviour?'

Bull's-eye!

'I could? Yes, I could. And I will. Miss Kendal, I would be delighted if you would give me a second chance to show you that I can be a ... a charming and attentive escort. Could we arrange another date?'

'I'm doing nothing this evening.'

'That's funny... neither am I.'

I couldn't believe this cheesy dialogue. I felt that at any minute we would go into our song. Than it struck me that Eve might be setting me up to get her own back.

'Are you quite sure you'd like to meet up?' I said earnestly.

'But not the cinema this time,' she said with a stern note in her voice. No doubt she had visions of being abandoned again in the dark with a scowling woman ranting about her corns.

'How about Lyon's Corner House, Piccadilly Circus, at eight this evening?'

'OK, but please be on time and promise not to run out on me once we've ordered a drink.'

'I promise.'

'In that case, I accept. I'll see you at eight.'

Before I could reply, she put the phone down.

At first I felt happy and pleased and then a doubt crept in. What if she really was getting her own back? What if she had me going to Lyon's and she didn't show. Or worse, she turned up and poured a cup of coffee over me before beating a hasty retreat. Well, it was something I'd have to risk.

I glanced at my watch. It was nearly five. I reckoned I'd time for a wash and shave ... no a bath, even if it meant running the gauntlet of the cranky geyser in the bathroom down the corridor. I needed to smell sweet. And to look good, too, which meant slipping into my best suit – well, my other suit to be precise. Then I'd still have time to visit Peter in hospital, have a morale-boosting whisky somewhere and be five minutes early at Lyon's Corner House for my date with the delicious Miss Kendal. Suddenly life felt a lot brighter than it had been as I'd viewed it a few hours ago.

I'd just got myself into my dressing-gown, towel over my arm and toilet bag in my mitt when the doorbell rang. Who the hell ...?

If it was a client, I'd tell them to come back in office hours. With some irritation, I pulled open the door, looking no doubt like a dodgy bath attendant.

My visitor was Leo Epstein.

He didn't bat an eyelid at my appearance. 'I think we'd better have a talk,' he said.

thirteen

I'd never interviewed a visitor to my office in my dressing gown before and although I felt somewhat vulnerable and ridiculous, I attempted to adopt an air of nonchalance as I offered Leo Epstein a chair and, popping my towel and toilet bag on the filing cabinet, I took up my usual position behind my desk.

Epstein looked nervous, quite different from the smooth, smug, silent fellow he had appeared the day before. Something had ruffled his oily feathers. I decided to play on this and I waited for him to start the ball rolling. With measured deliberation I extracted a cigarette from the packet and lit it, blowing the smoke sideways as I stared at my solicitor friend with interest.

'It's about Pamela Palfrey,' he said at last in a voice that was high and nervous.

'I thought it might be,' I smiled, taking another drag on my cigarette.

His hands fluttered to open his briefcase and he extracted a copy of that morning's *Daily Mirror*. It was open at page four and the blurred picture of the dead girl stared out at me. 'I recognized her picture in the paper this morning. A terrible business. Murdered.'

I nodded.

'I wasn't completely honest with you yesterday, I'm afraid,' he said gazing at me from under hooded lids.

'Oh?'

'Yes.' The eyes fluttered furiously with embarrassment. 'I knew Pamela somewhat more ... more intimately than I admitted.'

'You slept with her.'

Leo Epstein looked shocked. His brown skin paled and his jaw dropped. The truth has this effect on some people, especially when it takes the form of a confession.

'Just the once,' he added as some kind of exoneration.

'That in itself is not a crime, Mr Epstein. Indeed there were many men who slept with Pamela, so you are not alone. Tell me about it.'

He ran his long-fingered hand over his high forehead. 'She was working late one night and we got chatting. She was a very attractive girl, you know. It wasn't just her looks, it was the way she talked and moved. She had a very warm personality. I invited her into my office for a drink. It was harmless to begin with – at least I think it was. She got talking about how she dreamed of the better things in life. She was leading me on, I knew, and I was foolish enough to be led. Then she started playing with my tie and saying that there was nothing she wouldn't do to have some of my wealth. I knew what she meant. She was offering herself to me....'

'For money.'

Epstein turned his head sideways away from my gaze. 'Yes, I suppose you could put it like that.'

'No, let's only put it like that if it's true, Mr Epstein.' I steepled my fingers as he had done on the previous afternoon.

'Yes, it was for money. We made love on the rug in front of the fire in my office.'

'A sum of money changed hands.'

'One hundred pounds.'

I whistled. 'She didn't come cheap.'

'She wasn't cheap – not in the way you're suggesting. There was something very special about Pamela.'

'You got your money's worth then?'

Epstein flashed me an angry glance and his body tensed as though he were about to leap from the chair, probably to land one on me. That was no problem to me. I could handle myself but I reckoned he'd be more competent in smacking me with a writ rather than a left hook. And I wanted him riled; it would loosen his tongue further.

'I looked on the money as a gift rather than payment. And it was just the one occasion. It never happened again and neither of us alluded to the ... incident. The next day we just resumed the normal secretary and boss relationship.'

'That was rather strange.'

'I suppose so, but I think we both realized that we had crossed over a dangerous line and it was best to retreat as far back as possible.'

'Did you know that she slept with other men for money?'

Epstein shook his head. 'I didn't know – but I suppose I guessed she must. Her clothes and jewellery were too smart to have been bought on the salary I paid her.'

I stubbed my cigarette and leaned back in my chair. 'I see. Well, that's been very interesting, but why are you telling me all this?'

'Well, the last time we met it was just a case of a missing girl, but now it's murder....'

'And you're worried you'll be implicated.'

'Why, yes of course.'

'And it will become known that you sleep with your young secretaries.'

'Don't mock me, Hawke. I told you that this was just the one time anything like that had ever happened.'

'And you've regretted it ever since.'

He paused and threw me a wry smile. 'No, I have not. I have not. It was wonderful. She was wonderful. It is a treasured memory.'

He meant it too. The girl had really got under his skin. You could see it in his eyes. The more I learned about Pamela Palfrey the more I'd wished I'd met her. Immoral or at best amoral though she was, I was becoming fascinated by this creature.

'The question remains, why have you told me?'

'I don't expect you'll believe me, but now she's dead, I just wanted to tell someone, to share our secret. To set the record straight.'

'Wouldn't you be better telling the police rather than me, Mr Epstein?'

He looked away again. 'I hope it won't come to that. I had no connection with her once she'd left my employment. I was not involved with her at the time of her death. I cannot see how what happened between Pamela and myself has any bearing on her murder.'

'The police need the full picture to help them with their investigations. You can't withhold information like this.'

'But I've told *you*. Surely that's enough.' He was growing agitated now and his hands were flapping like an injured bird in his lap. 'This can have no connection with the murder of Pamela. Surely you can see that.'

'The fact that she slept with you for money before she left home may have a great bearing on matters. You cannot keep stum on this, Leo, old boy, you must bite the bullet and tell all.'

'I can't.'

I sighed in a theatrical fashion. 'Oh, yes you can and you will. Look, I'll give you twenty-four hours to contact the Yard – Inspector Knight's your man – or I'll have to do it for you. And the consequences of that will be far worse than spilling the beans yourself.'

Epstein shook his head in despair and got to his feet. 'I should never have come. I should never have told you.'

'You'll think differently when you've had chance to think about things. Confession is good for the soul.'

'Think about things!' he snapped. 'I've thought of nothing else since I saw her picture in the paper this morning.'

He made for the door.

'Don't forget Leo: twenty-four hours. Inspector Knight.'

My visitor swore and slammed the door behind him, rattling the pictures on the wall and rearranging the dust everywhere.

Well, I thought, when the vibrations had died away, another piece to my puzzle, but again one that does not join up with any other in any really meaningful way. Unless, of course, Mr Epstein was cleverer than I thought, and his story was some kind of smokescreen. I stored that observation away and continued with my ablutions.

*

Leo Epstein's visit had thrown my timetable into disarray. I realized that now everything had to be carried out at double speed if I was to get to Lyon's Corner House on time. God forbid that I was late. Certainly Eve would never forgive me. I doubt if *I'd* forgive myself. So I had to get ready in quick sticks. I had no sooner slipped my goose-pimpled body into the tepid waters and sloshed around in the rusty old container that professed to be a bath when I was out again, drying down my damp frame. A hurried, skimpy shave and then I was sloughing on my suit and knotting up my tie. A quick skim of the hair with the merest blob of Brylcreem to perk it up and I was ready.

It was nearly dark when I hit the streets and I was tempted to save time by taking a taxi to the Charing Cross Hospital but I decided to save money instead and walk. One never knew how expensive this night out might be. I didn't want to run out of cash just as it was getting interesting. However, I was able to shorten my journey by taking a direct route, more or less. This meant traversing a great number of side streets which occasionally ran out into one of the main thorough-fares – Oxford Street, Regent Street and The Haymarket – and then I slipped back into the maze. I was within a bandage's roll of the hospital, moving at a reasonable pace down Mitchum Street when I sensed that I was being followed. I just felt it. It's all very strange. I've heard other detectives say that you develop a sixth sense about it. I had no real proof at all except the soft footsteps I heard several yards behind me. And they could have belonged to some innocent pedestrian – but I just knew they didn't.

I avoided looking round in case I scared the feller off so I pretended that my shoelace was undone and knelt down to tie it up. Oh, I wish I hadn't. I wished I had turned round and scared him off. Kneeling down, I had put myself in a very vulnerable position. The next thing I knew I heard an angry cry and felt a blow to the back of my head. Someone switched on a vivid array of fairy lights which danced angrily before my eyes and I felt a searing pain. I fell face downwards, the cobbles seeming to enfold me in their stony embrace. I realized that I was losing consciousness as I struggled to catch a glimpse my attacker. All I saw was a dark shape with a scarf across the face. The bastard raised his weapon to strike again. I was too far gone to feel fear and too far gone to do anything but lie there. I just remember hearing a voice crying out in the darkness, 'Hi there, stop that!' before I slipped from this conscious world completely.

fourteen

How long I'd been in the blackness I didn't know but as I began to emerge once more into the light I was particularly aware of two things: Gene Krupa was practising a drum solo on my head and I was lying in a bed, the mattress of which was made out of concrete granules. I lay for some moments staring at the grey ceiling above me trying to get a hold back on my life.

Firstly, I told myself, let's be logical. Logical? I responded to myself somewhat heatedly, how can you get logical with that mad drummer belting away on your bonce? Just put him to the back of your mind, I replied smugly. He's already there, I snapped, and he's beating up a storm!

This surreal and groggy intercourse was interrupted by the arrival at my bedside of a woman in a nurse's uniform. That must be because she is a nurse, I told myself. And on this occasion I agreed with myself. And that must mean that you're in a hospital, I added with authority.

'Ah, you're awake. That's good,' the woman in the nurse's uniform said, turning my head gently to the side so she could examine the back. Gene Krupa upped the tempo.

'Mmm, you're still leaking a bit but it's not too bad. This dressing can stay on for now.'

'Leaking?' I asked, my mouth dry and cobwebby.

'You've had a nasty bump on the head, Mr Hawke, but we've X-rayed you and there's been no serious damage done. We've put a few stitches in just to make sure your brains don't drop out.' She smiled. 'You'll feel a little disorientated for a day or two but there's nothing to worry about. It's the usual after effect of concussion.'

'Can I get up now?'

'No you cannot. If you did, you'd fall down. You need a good night's rest before you'll be fit enough to get dressed.'

A dreadful thought suddenly struck me. 'What time is it?'

'Time?' she seemed nonplussed by this request. She consulted her watch clipped to the bosom of her uniform. 'It's half past eleven.'

'At night?'

'Of course.'

'Oh, bugger!' I cried.

'Now then, Mr Hawke, we won't have any talk like that in here.'

'I'm sorry, Nurse,' I said, closing my eye to the pain and disappointment of the real world. She wasn't to know that I'd gone and done it again. I'd left Eve in the lurch for the second time. Whatever was a worse consistency than mud, my name was it. Briefly, I had a vision of Eve sitting alone at a table in Lyon's Corner House, repeatedly sticking a hat pin into a little male figure fashioned out of a doughnut. That doughnut man was me.

The nurse's voice broke my wild reverie. 'Can I get you anything? A cup of tea perhaps.'

'I suppose a double whisky is out of the question.'

She gave me a smile. 'It is. You'll have a big enough hangover in the morning without the help of Mr Johnnie Walker.'

'A cup of tea it is then and some water please. I'm very dry.'

'I'll see what I can do.'

My Florence Nightingale bustled off and as she did so I saw that there were screens around my bed. I was isolated from the rest of the ward. Perhaps my concussion was contagious.

When the nurse returned sometime later she had a cup of tea, a carafe of water and a plate of biscuits. 'I've brought you some bourbons,' she said with a grin. 'You strike me as a chocolate bourbon man.'

I smiled back. 'I'm more of a Kentucky bourbon man.'

We struggled together to get me into a sitting position. She was on the plumpish side and not particularly pretty, but somehow in my bedraggled state I found the closeness of her very sensuous. She smelled of lavender and her skin was smooth and warm. She aroused a spark in me which in my current mental state should have been dormant. Acting on impulse, I kissed her on the cheek.

'Now, now, Mr Hawke, don't you start something you know you definitely can't finish,' she warned me with a twinkle in her eye.

'Sorry, Nurse.'

'I should think so too. Now drink your tea, eat your biccies and then get a good night's rest.'

'I will, I will, but before you go could you tell me how I got here. I presume this is Charing Cross Hospital?'

She nodded. 'Are you sure you want to deal with this now?'

'I'm sure,' I said, biting on a bourbon.

'A chap brought you in. Says you were hit from behind and he managed to scare off the attacker before he could do any more damage. He then dragged you into casualty. Luckily you weren't far away.'

'What was this chap's name?'

She shook her head. 'Don't know. He disappeared before anyone could get his name. Just a passer-by I guess,'

'I guess.'

'Looks like you'll never get to know who your good Samaritan was.'

After the nurse had gone, I tried to remember the moments just before I lost consciousness but my brain wasn't up to it. But one thing was clear to me. If Mr Samaritan hadn't acted as he did, I could easily be in another part of this hospital, on a slab with a white sheet over my face.

It was a different nurse who roused me from my dreamless slumbers. She was grey-haired and elderly, no doubt brought out of retirement for the duration. She had 'no nonsense' written all over her severe features. 'Now then, I'm Nurse

Williams and I'm here to change your dressing, young man, so no fuss please. Sit up, lean forward and let me get on with it.'

I did as I was told. With gentle, nimble fingers she removed the pad from my wound and laid it in a dish on the bedside cabinet. It was curved and crusted with dried blood, like a small scarlet crab.

'Oh, that's coming along just fine,' she murmured, as she applied the new dressing to my wounded bonce. 'You'll live.'

'I'm glad to hear it.'

'Right, that's me done. Breakfast in half an hour and the doctor will be on the ward around ten.'

'That's all very well,' I said with a grimace, 'but I don't think my bladder will wait that long.'

'OK, I'll get one of the duty nurses to provide you with a bottle.'

'No, no. I'd like to … to go on my own.'

She tut-tutted me, but grabbed a dressing-gown from the bedside cabinet. 'Let's see if you can stand up before you try to wee, eh?'

My body felt as though it hadn't been used for a decade and my head throbbed as though it might explode, but with Nurse Williams's help I got myself out of bed and was able to stand more or less erect.

'How do you feel?' she asked, as she held the dressing-gown for me to navigate my arms into it.

'I'll manage,' I said through gritted teeth. I did feel rough, but I was determined not to be incapacitated by a bump on the head, however nasty. I couldn't wait around for the doctor to suggest I stay in hospital another day. I had things to do – a murder to solve. I had to get out of here. Nurse Williams guided me towards the lavatories. I felt part zombie, part geriatric and I certainly excited some interest with the other patients who gazed at me over their well folded linen sheets thinking I'd escaped from a Boris Karloff movie.

'I can make my own way back,' I said, on reaching the frosted door which announced 'Gentlemen's Lavatories'.

My guide nodded and left me to it. Once I had relieved myself, I took a gander at my mug in the mirror over the sink. I looked like I'd been on an all night bender for a week. My skin was pale and blotchy and there was a dark ring under my good eye which made me look as though I'd been using one of those joke telescopes that have a sooty substance round the eyepiece. I swilled my face in cold water and dampened down my unruly hair. If only I could have shaved and cleaned my teeth.

I stretched and bent over, trying to rev up my body engine. It responded nicely but my head still felt as though someone had sliced off the back of it. By the time I emerged on to the corridor, I was feeling a little more human. I tried to put a spring in my step as I passed by my fellow patients but they had lost interest in me.

Once behind the screens, I searched for my clothes. My best suit, mud-stained and torn at the knees, was crumpled up in the locker by my bedside cabinet, as was the rest of my clobber. Like a ballet dancer in slow motion I dressed myself, grimacing and groaning softly in the process. Never has it taken a man longer to put on his underpants and trousers – or tie up his shoes. Every time I bent over, my head pounded and my vision blurred.

After what seemed hours, I was ready to make my escape. Peering out from the screens, I could see no members of the medical Gestapo in view, so I slipped out quietly and made my way towards the exit doors. One old cove caught sight of me as I hurried by stiffly and he turned to a fellow patient in the next bed with the news, 'I think that chap is doin' a bunk.'

A bunk is what I did and I felt better for it. I hate hospitals and I hate being cooped up anywhere. I followed my nose until I saw a sign which gave various directions. I headed for the children's ward.

There was a new porter on duty outside the boy's room. He eyed me suspiciously, as well he might.

'I've come to see Peter,' I said lightly with a smile.

'Have you now? And who might you be?' His expression, glum and wary, never changed.

'I'm a friend.'

'Bit old for being a friend of the nipper in there, ain't you?'

'The police have given permission for me to visit him. Inspector Llewellyn arranged it.'

'Did he now?'

'Yes. You could ask sister.'

As luck would have it, just at that moment the door of the room opened and a man I took to be a doctor emerged. Well, the white coat and stethoscope rather gave the game away. He looked at me with the same degree of suspicion as the porter. 'What is it, Whittaker?' he asked the surly sentry.

'This ... gentleman says he wants to see the boy.'

The doctor gave me a further examination. 'You look as though you've been in the wars yourself.'

'A little case of concussion, that's all. I'm fine.' I repeated my request and when I mentioned David's name and Scotland Yard, the doctor smiled and nodded. 'Oh, yes, I know about you.'

'So, can I see Peter?'

The doctor bit his lower lip. 'I suppose so, but he's still not properly conscious. The fever has worsened. He's having it rough, poor lad.'

'He will pull through, won't he?'

'It's unlikely that he won't.'

This circumspect reply did little to reassure me.

'Come on then, just for a minute.' The doctor ushered me into the room and then I followed.

Standing by the bedside, I gazed down at Peter, his face flushed feverous red and shiny with perspiration, his head lolling from side to side as he mumbled something. It saddened my heart to see the poor lad in such a condition. I knelt down by him. 'What is it, old chap?' I said softly.

His eyes flickered open. 'I saw him ... I saw him,' he croaked. I couldn't tell whether Peter was responding to my question or not. His brow contracted and his mouth tightened as though whatever was going through his fevered mind frightened him. 'I saw him,' he said again, his voice clearer this time. 'Blood ... blood ... blood on his hands. I saw him.'

'Who did you see? Peter? Who did you see?'

He leaned forward, his eyes staring fixedly at me. 'Tiger Blake,' he said. 'I saw Tiger Blake.'

fifteen

This time I did take a taxi. I reckoned that the trek back to
Hawke Towers would just about do me in, so within
minutes of leaving the confines of Charing Cross Hospital, I
was in a jaunty taxi being chauffeured to my home. I also had
managed to pick up a paper and I skimmed it during the
journey for news on the Palfrey/Palmer case. I found what I was
looking for in a small item on page four. The police had now
arrested 'the prostitute's boyfriend, Samuel Fraser, an actor, and
charged him with her murder. Detective Chief Inspector Alan
Knight assured reporters that he was confident of a conviction
when the case came to trial'.

So the thick-headed, short-sighted, blinkered bombast had
followed his huge proboscis, the one with the blocked nostrils,
and gone for the obvious suspect and got an easy arrest. Case
closed and a pat on the back for Knight. That was really bad
news for Fraser. There would be no more official police investigation into the case with the result that the real culprit would
get away. No doubt he or she would have read the news with a
great sigh of relief. So, Johnny, boy, I told myself, it really was
up to you now to nail the bastard. Easier said than done, of
course for I had to admit I was really little wiser than old Dirty
Knight. Those puzzle pieces were growing in number but not in
clarity. I wondered if Mr Gordon Moore aka Tiger Blake really
fitted into the frame. It certainly seemed that he was one of
Pammie's clients. And what about Peter's fevered utterances
about seeing Tiger Blake with blood on his hands? Of course,
he'd watched the film a few nights before and it was probably
images from the movie which had stayed in his mind. But I'd

seen it, too, and I knew there was no scene in which Tiger had blood on his hands.

Once I got home, I brewed myself a strong cup of tea and rustled up some slices of toast and devoured them with the savage voracity of a cave man who hadn't eaten a breast of pterodactyl for months. After a wash and shave, and a soothing Craven A I was beginning to feel half human again. I examined my dressing with the use of two mirrors. It was dry with no sign of blood seeping through the gauze, so I was obviously on the mend. I grinned back at myself in the mirror. A cock-eyed Boris Karloff stared back at me with the same grin.

Then I planned the rest of my day. There were a few things I wanted to check out. Again, I would have to use a taxi. I still didn't feel energetic enough to tramp across London. I looked in my wallet: the Palfrey advance was gradually dwindling. Still, I would survive.

I got a cab to Regent's Terrace and walked along to the building where Pammie Palmer had her flat. As I suspected, there was no policeman on duty now. With the case being closed, solved, done and dusted, and the hangman polishing his rope, there was no need to keep the flat under surveillance. I went inside the building, rode up in the rickety lift to the third floor and knocked innocently on the door. I knew there would be no reply but I had to check. After my third attempt, I felt happy. It was good to know there was an empty flat there waiting to be scrutinized.

It is amazing what you can do to a lock with a piece of wire, some know-how and a fair bit of patience. It was one of the tricks I learned when I first went on the beat. A grizzled sergeant who'd seemed old enough to have been one of the original Bow Street runners took a shine to me and showed me the procedure. Since then I always carried a short length of strong wire in my wallet. Kneeling down by the keyhole, I set to work. After five minutes of twisting and scraping, I heard the satisfying click of the lock bar slipping back. Open Sesame. Eat your heart out, Mr Houdini.

Mopping my damp brow, I entered the apartment. The first thing that struck me was how tiny it was. Smart and chic certainly but on a doll's house scale. The entrance hall ran the length of the flat with two rooms on either side. The first one, on the left, was the sitting room. It was sparsely and stylishly furnished but had no personality stamped on it. Signs of the recent police presence were in evidence: the carpet had been pulled back in one corner, drawers were open, most of them empty, as were the ashtrays. The locust squad had obviously been fairly thorough. It looked as though I had been consigned to the role of Detective Mother Hubbard. This impression was confirmed as I mooched around the room, lifting cushions and peering behind picture frames: the cupboard was bare.

I crossed the hall and into the bedroom. It was a windowless room so I switched on the light. The bed had been stripped and all bed linen removed but there was a dark-crimson stain on the mattress to bear witness to murder. The blood of Pammie Palmer. I always found something unnerving about a room in which someone has died, particularly one who has died violently. There's an unnatural chill and a hissing silence in the air which assail your senses. I didn't want to stay here long and looking around I reckoned there was little point anyway. Again drawers had been emptied and left hanging open like lolling wooden tongues and, as I suspected, the wardrobe had been raided, the clothes no doubt having been bagged up by the lads or maybe the ladies of Scotland Yard. I never expected Knight's bunch to have been this thorough. Although now they had charged Sam Fraser, no doubt all the items they had acquired would be regarded as unnecessary evidence and squirrelled away without examination in a dark corner of Scotland Yard. The pity of it.

Some strange instinct made me touch the bed, my fingers running across the mattress towards the patch of dried blood. I wasn't a stranger to death or to murder but I never felt comfortable with it. The enormity of one person taking another's life – for whatever reason – chilled me to the marrow. How deep into the dark forests of the night does one have to go before one can summon up sufficient strength and malevolence to commit murder? I didn't want to know the answer.

I took one last look round and was about to leave when I noticed a note pad on the bedside table by the telephone. On further inspection, I saw that the pad was blank, but as I leaned over it to examine it, I caught sight of something white that had slipped down the back of the table. I pulled it away from the wall to discover that one of the sheets from the pad had slipped down there. It had been missed by the locust squad.

With a dry mouth and beating heart, I picked up the paper. It had numbers on it. A telephone number – unless I was woefully mistaken. I gave the sheet a little kiss and sat on the bed and dialled the number. The phone rang and rang. I waited. It rang and rang. I gave it two minutes but still it rang. Well, it appears they are out then, Johnny boy, whoever they are, I told myself.

I was just about to replace the receiver when miraculously it was picked up at the other end. Initially I was assailed by a bout of violent coughing and then a rough male voice bellowed down the wires, ''Allo!'

'Hello,' I replied cheerily. 'Who is that speaking?'

'Who wants ter know?'

'This is John Hawke. I ... er ... I was wanting to speak to Mr Chaplin.' I made the name up on the spur of the moment and I suddenly had a vision of the little tramp with the bowler hat and cane.

'Well, this ain't him. My name's not Chaplin.'

'Oh, dear,' I said, apologetically. 'What address is that?'

'Are you trying to be funny, mate? This is no bloomin' address. It's a ruddy phone box. I've been waiting outside for nigh on two minutes waiting for it to stop ringing so I can call my missus.'

A phone box!

'I'm awfully sorry,' I said, not wanting to increase this fellow's indignation any more. 'I'll get off the line straight away so that you can call your missus but would you be kind enough to tell me where the box is?'

'It's on the corner of Berner's Street and Boynton Street. That do you?'

'Thank you, Mr ...?'

'Never you mind who.'

And the phone went dead.

When I hit the street again, I was glad of the fresh air. For some moments I stood on the pavement taking deep breaths, expunging the air of death from my lungs. The fresh supply of oxygen must have rushed to my brain nourishing and energizing it for something clicked up there in my rather sore *medulla oblongata*. As I stood with my back to the building which housed Pammie Palmer's flat, I realized for the first time that I was facing Regent's Park. The railings, the trees, you dummy! Yes, that's Regent's Park. And it was in Regent's Park where young Peter was found camping out. Young Peter who rambled deliriously about seeing Tiger Blake with blood on his hands. I turned my head to look at the block of flats and then back again to Regent's Park. I shouldn't have moved my head so quickly, not in my rather delicate recuperative state. My vision blurred and I staggered back against the railings, grabbing them for support.

I must have seemed drunk to the elderly lady passing by for she gave me a wide berth and a nasty look. I didn't care. I had made a connection. If Tiger Blake, aka Gordon Moore, had visited Pammie on the night of her death, had murdered her in fact, he could have been seen leaving the building by Peter from some hidey-hole in the park. And if Moore had murdered Pammie – a vision of that stained mattress flashed into my mind – then he may well have had blood on his hands. Suddenly some of those puzzle pieces were beginning to slip into place.

sixteen

'There is only one way to get out of here ... and that's by killing the guards.'

The beautiful blonde girl blanched and her bosom heaved, straining against her sweat-soaked shirt. 'But how?' she squealed. 'They've got your gun.'

Tiger Blake clenched his teeth and with a deft movement extracted a cruel-looking knife from the top of one of his riding boots. It flashed in the light. 'This should do the trick,' he grinned and then froze.

'Cut! That's a print,' came a voice beyond the lights.

'Thank the fuck for that,' observed Tiger Blake in uncharacteristic fashion. Turning his back on his leading lady he walked out of the prison cell on to the studio floor.

'That's fine, Gordon,' said director Norman Lee. 'We shan't need you again till after lunch. It's the interrogation scene. You've had the rewrites?'

Tiger Blake, who had now fully metamorphosed into the actor Gordon Moore, gave Lee a sour nod. 'They're always fucking changing things.'

'For a better picture,' said Lee with a pleasant grin. After six films together he was used to Gordon's moods and was adept at dealing with them. Lee was an American Jew, an escapee from Z pictures on Hollywood's Poverty Row to British B movies which satisfied his modest ambitions. He was a strong believer in the quiet life and in this instance he knew that *Tiger Blake's Arabian Adventure* was the last feature they would make together so he was happy to let the actor have his way. Once the film was completed, he could say goodbye to shoddy

Tiger Blake and, more importantly, goodbye to the awkward bastard who played him. 'Nice work this morning,' he added, tapping Moore's arm. He knew how to be oleaginous when it was necessary. 'Three o'clock on set please.'

Moore gave him a brief nod and departed for his dressing-room.

Lee hoped that his star didn't down too much gin before the interrogation scene. The dialogue was fairly tricky and they'd been lucky enough to get Francis L. Sullivan to play Ben Zahir, the chief of police. Now he was a real actor.

Moore shut the door of his dressing-room and leaned against it. He could feel tears begin to well in his eyes and he forced them back. He didn't want to have to redo his make-up again. It took longer than ever these days to make a flabby 48-year-old look ten years younger. Yes, it took longer and the results were far from convincing. He hated growing old. He hated being stuck with the Tiger Blake image – but it was all he'd got. And it had made him a household name. This was the first movie in which he'd had to wear a toupee. His own sandy hair had thinned so much that his bald patch could not be disguised with careful combing any more. Well, it won't be for much longer. This was the last Tiger Blake. The scrap heap was waiting.

He poured himself a large gin and guzzled half of it in one gulp. It burned his throat and it pleased him. He wrapped a thin dressing-gown around him and lay on the couch nursing the replenished glass of gin between his hands. He'd take a nap and then look at those fucking rewrites.

As he closed his eyes, the vision of Pammie Palmer's lovely face filled the dark vacuum. Her mouth was open in a silent scream and her eyes glowered back at him in a glassy, accusative stare. The image held for a moment as Moore's body stiffened with apprehension and then suddenly the girl's eyes blinked, blood seeped from the corners of her mouth and the scream was no longer silent: it was a shrill and insistent whine. She reached out to touch him.

Moore opened his eyes, banishing the image. He gave a grunt of fear and sat bolt upright on the couch, a fine film of perspiration bathing his brow. As he caught his breath, he realized that the scream was in fact his telephone, which rang with a high-pitched nagging tone. Taking another gulp of gin, he snatched up the receiver.

'Yes,' he snarled.

'Mr Moore, it's Tristan here....'

'How many times have I told you, you pansy, not to disturb me between takes?'

'I know sir, I know. But this is rather important. It's an urgent personal call.'

'It's not my wife, is it?'

'No, sir. It's a call from a business associate, a Miss Pammie Palmer.'

Gordon Moore dropped his glass of gin which shattered as it hit the tiled floor.

'Shall I put her through, Mr Moore?'

The actor's mind was in a whirl. His throat was dry and constricted when he replied some seconds later.

'Yes, put her through.' For a moment he wondered if this was real or a vivid dream.

There was a brief silence followed by some crackling on the line – but no one spoke, forcing the actor to speak first. 'Hello.'

'Gordon.' The voice was low, almost a whisper, and strangely devoid of humanity.

'Who is this?'

'I know what you did, Gordon. You have blood on your hands, Gordon.'

Moore gripped the receiver tight. 'What are you talking about? Who is this? What do you want?'

'What do I want? I want justice, Gordon. I want you.'

And then the line went dead leaving the searing sound of buzzing in his ears.

Like a man in a trance, he replaced the receiver. He sat on the couch and put his head in his hands, not caring this time how much he disturbed his make-up. 'Oh, my God,' he said despairingly. 'Oh, my God.'

seventeen

Here I was back in Bermondsey, but this time I wasn't going to venture into Mr Leo Epstein's emporium – I'd had enough of the old smoothy yesterday. However I was reminded that I ought to get in touch with Dirty Knight to let him know of lovely Leo's involvement with Pammie – not that I suspected that he would be the least bit interested in the information now that he'd made an arrest. I felt sure that if someone walked into Knight's office and confessed to the crime, offering up the weapon with the girl's blood on it, he'd smile and say, 'Thanks for your help, but we have the matter in hand already. Just leave your name with the desk sergeant.' It was characters like Knight, coppers with closed minds and naked ambition, who made me glad that I was no longer on the force. I couldn't work like that. Thanks to the army, I didn't have to. Although it would be nice to have the regular income that came with the job. And both eyes, of course.

I found myself a cosy doorway virtually opposite Epstein's place in which to wait. I wanted to catch Eve as she left work and see if I could convince her that fate, rather than my own fecklessness, in the form of a bloke with a blunt instrument had stepped in the way of my meeting her the previous evening. At least I had a sound piece of evidence in my bandaged head. She could take off the dressing and inspect the wound if that's what was needed to do the job.

I lit up a Craven A and leaned against the wall, inhaling deeply. It was just after quarter to five. I reckoned Epstein would release her about five or maybe half past. On reflection it would be half past. He was the type to keep 'em at the grindstone as long as possible. Before making the trek to Bermondsey – by tube this time for not only was I beginning to feel my old self again but I also had an inclination to rub shoulders with living breathing humanity after being alone in the murder flat – I'd traipsed round to the corner of Berner's Street and Boynton Street to visit my suspect phone box. It didn't have much to say for itself. It was just a normal red phone box, rather shabby inside with the usual mechanical gubbins. Out of a childhood habit I pressed button B a couple of times but it just clanked in a negative fashion and failed to release any of its treasures. Typically there was an interesting selection of tab ends littering the floor and the air stank of sweat and other unpleasantnesses. Nothing out of the ordinary at all. So at first glance it looked rather like a dead end. Then I got to thinking why Pammie had written the phone number down in the first place. Surely the only reason was that so she could contact someone in the box – someone who was waiting for the call. There couldn't have been anything random about it. But why here? Why a public phone box?

The buildings in the area housed offices – there were no private dwellings – and down Boynton Street there was the Corona, a gentleman's club. In other words, all establishments in the vicinity would have their own phones for the use of employees and members. There would be no need to pop out to a telephone box – unless, of course, you needed to be sure of absolute privacy, to be sure that you were not being overheard, overheard telephoning a prostitute.

But, wait a minute – she rang *him*. Or more likely rang him back because he ran out of coppers. Oh, John Hawke, you beamish boy, you are functioning on all cylinders again. My eye turned towards the green canopy which advertised itself as the Corona, a club for gentlemen who carry cheque books rather than cash and the only folk around at night.

Snap. I heard another piece of the puzzle snuggle into place.

· I wandered along the pavement and approached the club. As I mounted the steps, a green-liveried commissionaire stepped forward out of the shadows. He looked as though he was chewing a sour lemon especially for my benefit.

'Can I help you, sir?' His tone was sepulchral, carrying its own tomb-like echo.

I felt like clutching my forelock and mumbling, 'I've come to see the young master', but instead I said, 'How does one get inside?'

'One becomes a member, sir.'

'Ah. And how does one become a member?'

'You must be proposed by two existing members.'

I nodded judiciously. 'Sounds fair. Could I see a list of existing members so I can choose who I'd like to recommend me?'

'I'm afraid not, sir. That information can only be divulged to existing members.'

I frowned. 'Then how ...?'

'You need to be personally recommended, sir.'

'Couldn't you recommend me?'

'But I don't know you, sir.'

'Well, I don't know you, but I don't mind. You look like a decent sort of bloke....'

The eyes flashed with irritation. I knew it was time to leave.

'Never mind,' I said casually. 'I bet you never get Tommy Carter's group in to blow up a storm. I think I'll stick to The Velvet Cage.'

Rather like a dignified, elderly cuckoo in a Swiss clock the commissionaire slipped back into the shadows.

It was now 5.15 and the lights were still blazing in the Epstein empire. I was here for the duration. As I lit up my second cigarette, I pondered on the telephone box and the Corona Club. Certainly Pammie Palmer was more high-class courtesan than common prosser, providing sexual favours to the well heeled rather than the likes of me – in fact, just the sort of bloke who hibernates behind the doors of the Corona Club. And wasn't it likely that if Corona Charlie wanted to arrange a liaison at Pammie's place, he'd rather do it in private? In the protected confines of the nearest call box? You never know who might hear you in the club. Sound may well travel further in a refined atmosphere! I knew I was constructing this scenario with a fair amount of supposition but it worked logically. However, if I were correct in my assumptions, where did that leave me? Not a lot closer to learning the truth about the girl's death. Even if Corona Charlie had rung her on the night of the murder – run out of change and then asked her to ring him back – that's not to say he saw her that night or visited the flat … or murdered her. He could only be a vague suspect, no more.

It was 5.30 and quite dark now but still slave-driver Epstein had not shut up shop. The blackout curtains had been drawn, but I could still observe the suffused glow of the electric lighting at the edges of the window. Suddenly I felt tired and depressed. For all my efforts over the last couple of days, in reality I was still on the starting line waiting for that damn pistol to go off.

At 5.40 the office lights went out and I waited with apprehension for Eve to make her appearance. When she did so, she was accompanied by another girl, a tall blonde-haired, full-bodied young lady whose face, I could tell even at fifty paces and in the gloom, had not been spared the full make-up treatment – she was coated in it. Of course, I realized, she must be Pammie's replacement, chosen specially by Leo for her office skills and typing speed – naturally. The two girls appeared to be in animated conversation.

I crossed the road and approached the pair. God knew what I was going to say. *I* certainly didn't. I hadn't a clue. In the end I came out with the highly original, 'Hello, Eve.'

For a moment she was nonplussed, as I suppose I would be if I had been approached in the dusk by someone I'd only met twice before. However, she soon regained her composure.

'Goodbye,' she snapped in response to my greeting, and grabbed hold of her companion's arm. 'Come on, Dawn.'

I stepped in front of them. 'Look, I'm sorry about last night but I can explain.'

'Chasing another fugitive from justice were we?' She arched an accusative eyebrow.

'Well, no....'

'Whatever the reason ... the excuse ... I just don't want to know. Now leave me alone.' She was very angry and very beautiful.

'Please, don't be like this, Eve. At least let me explain and then if you want me to go ... I'll go. I'll never darken your doorstep again.'

'I'm just not interested, Mr Hawke. To be stood up once is bad enough, but twice....'

Dawn eyed me up, fluttering her heavily mascaraed eyelids like batwings. 'Oh, give him a chance, Evie. He seems ever so nice.'

Thank you for the vote of confidence, painted lady.

'That's what I thought the first time I saw him. Appearances can be deceptive. Now do come on, Dawn.'

It was time for drastic action. I whipped off my hat and swivelled round so they could see the dressing on the back of my head. 'I was nearly killed last night,' I cried.

It did the trick. I heard both women gasp at the sight of the wound.

I turned round to face them again. 'I was on my way to meet you, Eve, when I was hit from behind by a vicious blow and left for dead.' I placed extra emphasis on the words 'vicious' and 'dead'.

Eve's features softened, while Dawn was almost in tears. 'You poor man,' said Dawn, reaching out and touching my arm.

'This isn't some kind of trick is it?' asked the more canny Eve.

I shook my head violently and then feigned another grimace of pain. 'You can check with the Charing Cross Hospital, if you like. I spent the night there in Ward 14.'

'I may well do that,' replied Eve with a glimmer of a smile.

'Please let me make it up to you. Could I take you for a meal tonight and a club afterwards?'

What was I saying? The moths in my wallet were old enough to vote.

Dawn came to my support. 'Oh go on, Evie, give the little hero another chance.' She beamed at me, her broad crimson lips leaving a lipstick trail across her teeth. 'I would.' She gave me a look. That look.

Gently, Eve disentangled her arm from Dawn's. 'There'd better be no running off this time, Johnny Hawke or....' Really she was lost for what suitable consequences would result from such an eventuality but I didn't care now, I'd got another chance.

'If Hermann Goerring came into the restaurant, I wouldn't give him a second glance,' I said.

Both girls laughed.

'Very well,' said Eve with mock reluctance, 'if Dawn doesn't mind. We were going for a drink and a sandwich at the pub down the road.'

More fluttering of batwings. 'Oh, don't be silly. You get off with your young man. I'll make do with some Spam and chips at home,' said Dawn generously. Very generously, not only was she giving up the chance of having a girlie chat over a nice gin and tonic and a nice sandwich but she was prepared to go home eat Spam instead! Greater love hath no girl but to give up her night out for a plate of processed meat.

And so, ten minutes later, Eve and I were speeding in a taxi towards the West End. I'd had to do some rapid thinking in the meantime. I had blurted out my invitation to a meal and a club in desperation without consulting my brain or, more importantly, my wallet. The only way I was going to work this was to head for The Velvet Cage. I was on friendly terms with Tony the head waiter there and with luck he'd let me have a couple of dinners buckshee, and similarly I could wangle a few drinks from Jimmy the bartender. I knew all this would cost me later, but looking at Eve's face again, I reckoned it was worth it.

eighteen

On our taxi journey I told Eve about the boy Peter and my visit to the hospital and how I had been attacked. By the time I'd finished my tale of woe she was looking sympathetic and concerned and, although she didn't hold my hand, she sat very close to me. She was warm and smelled fresh with a faint hint of perfume. I wanted to kiss her.

'Why do you think you were attacked?'

I gave a shrug – the sort that Jimmy Cagney gives when he wants to indicate that something is of no consequence. 'Hazard of the job,' I said drily.

'But there must be a reason. Don't you have any ideas at all? A list of suspects.'

If I did, darling, your boss may well be top of the list.

'Not really,' I said. 'Things are a little vague at the moment.'

'Has this anything to do with Pammie's murder?'

'I shouldn't think so,' I lied. At this stage of the investigation I intended to keep all my cards clamped tightly to my chest. 'Look, Eve, let's forget about this business for tonight and just enjoy ourselves. I need a little break from crime for an hour or two. What d'you say?'

'If that's what you want, but I am interested ... concerned.'

Concerned! My heart did a flip.

As expected, Tony the head waiter at The Velvet Cage turned up trumps. I had a whispered word with him while Eve was depositing her coat in the cloakroom. The little Italian grinned. 'For you, this once. But once only. If the boss find out he'll have my guts for gasmasks.'

I grinned back. I loved the way Tony mangled the English language. He would have been a wow on the radio. In fact he sounded like a character from 'ITMA'.

'You couldn't throw in a bottle of Chianti, too?'

He closed his eyes in mock disgust. 'How far you like me to chuck it? If you like I arrange a Royce Rolls to take you home as well!'

'Good man.' I put my arm round his shoulders and gave him a squeeze.

He disentangled himself at speed. 'One thing, Johnny One Note. I expect a good tip.'

'I'll do what I can.'

At that point, Eve came into view. She was wearing a neat little two piece costume. It was her work clothes, but she had the sort of figure and presence that transcended the simplicity of the outfit.

Tony's eyes widened. 'Your date?' He nodded in Eve's direction.

'Yup.'

'She's some lady. Very classy. I make sure the meal is extra good.'

'You're the tops, Tony.'

'I know,' he said, bowing as Eve joined us. 'Good evening, madam. Come this way Mr Hawke and your lovely lady, I have a very special table for you.'

This was Tony's usual routine. According to him, every table in the joint was 'a special table'.

The club wasn't particularly full that evening, although it was still early and the richer clients dined later. There was a group of officers enjoying their leave in a lively fashion and several middle-aged couples struggling to converse with each other, along with a few dodgy characters, some of whom I knew by sight and some I knew personally. One, Soapy Sam Dawson, king of the spivs – 'you want it, I can get it, my son, for a consideration, of course' – made a point of passing by the table. 'Looks like a nasty knock to the bonce you got there, Johnny boy,' he leered.

'I got out of bed too quickly this morning.'

He glanced at Eve and then back to me. 'Now that was a very rash thing to do, my boy. I hope you didn't disturb the lady.' He winked and was on his way.

I looked at Eve and gave an embarrassed shrug. 'Characters you meet in my line of business,' I said sheepishly.

She just giggled at my discomfort.

The meal was the best I'd had in ages. It wasn't particularly good but nevertheless it was the best I'd had in ages. At least the gravy wasn't transparent and the chicken did not have the consistency of a raffia mat. But the food was incidental to my real enjoyment of the evening which was being with Eve Kendal. I am too inarticulate to explain why exactly I found her so attractive, apart from her looks, but I felt completely at ease with her which for a fellow who is usually uneasy and ham-fisted around good-looking women is just short of a miracle. How can you have pleasant conversations without actually saying anything of consequence? I couldn't say, I just know that we did that evening.

However after the plates were cleared and we were on to the coffee and brandies, a little professional light went on in the back of my head which alerted me to the idea that I really should be doing a little detective work here. I was aware I'd said that I didn't want to think about work for a while but despite how much I was enjoying myself, the whole matter of Pammie Palmer's murder kept slipping into my mind. And, apart from being absolutely scrumptious, Eve was a valuable source of information.

'Has Lustful Leo Epstein ever made advances to you?' I asked, as casually as I could, while I lit my first post-prandial cigarette. I was conscious that this was a severe conversational gear change and Eve's frown informed me that I had somewhat dampened the mood. What was I saying about being ham-fisted?

She gave me a wry smile. 'I've been there four years and Leo approaches me on average once a year. But then he approaches all the girls he employs at some time. Some have left because of his pestering.'

'Not you though.'

'I can handle him.'

'You've never been tempted.'

'He's not my type.'

'You have a type?'

She grinned and gave me a knowing look. 'Possibly.'

'What about Pammie? Did she fall for the charms of Mr Epstein?'

'Rather the other way about. He was besotted by her.'

'Really? How did she react?'

'Pammie always went with the flow if there was money involved.'

I nodded. That was as accurate a character reference as you could get on dear Pammie. 'Would it surprise you to know that on one occasion she slept with Mr Epstein?'

Eve raised her eyebrows. 'On one occasion? It would surprise me. I think the phrase is "quite frequently".'

Now it was my turn to raise my eyebrows. 'They were having an affair?'

Eve rolled her glass in a circular motions, swilling the brandy around inside and then taking a gentle sip. 'I've never quite understood the word affair and what emotions are involved. I do know that Pammie went with Leo on a regular basis but I'm fairly sure it wasn't for love.'

'You didn't tell me this when I came to the office,' I said gently.

'I didn't know you quite as well then. I didn't think it had any real bearing on Pammie's disappearance. Is that what you think?' She gulped down the last of her brandy.

What I thought was that old Epstein had difficulty with the truth. It would seem that his little confession to me about falling by the wayside just the once was only part of a much longer and probably more complex story. By throwing me a crumb of the much larger loaf he hoped to escape further scrutiny. Well, he was wrong.

'I'm not sure,' I told Eve casually, 'but all information is useful in building up a full picture.'

'Well, I can tell you this affair, if you want to call it that, fizzled out some months ago. I think Epstein got fed up with buying her presents and doling out cash for so little in return. I think he wanted to take matters further.'

'What, you mean marriage?'

'Possibly; he was that smitten. He was very cut up when Pammie resisted taking their relationship any further.'

I said nothing and sipped my brandy.

'Now, Johnny, can we drop the subject? I thought we were here to enjoy ourselves.'

I nodded. 'Yeah, you're right. Let's go through and listen to some jazz. You like jazz?'

Eve wrinkled her nose. 'I prefer Ambrose or Henry Hall really.'

'Hey, kid, you ain't heard nothing until you hear the Tommy Parker quartet.'

Eve giggled. The wine and the brandy had made her a little tipsy. 'Convince me.'

We found a little table to the left of the bandstand and sat down halfway through Tommy's trumpet solo on 'Pennies from Heaven'. Tommy was a competent player who fancied himself as Harry James but he lacked his smooth clarity of tone and adventurous spirit to be considered in the same class. After a version of 'You're the Top' played at a remarkably slow tempo, Tommy introduced Beulah White, who straight away launched into a scat version of 'S'wonderful'.

'You think she could have learned the words,' giggled Eve, her eyes glazing and her lids drooping.

'Time you went home, young lady,' I said.

'You could be right.'

The onslaught of cold air that greeted us as we left the club seemed at first to accelerate Eve's inebriation. I grabbed her arm to steady her and she gave me an affectionate peck on the cheek. I attempted to return the compliment but she pulled back and looked away. With a shrug, I hailed a cab.

'I'll see you home,' I said, as the taxi pulled up by the kerb.

'No, no. I can see myself....' She disentangled herself from me and tottered towards the cab door.

'It's no trouble, Eve. I think I should go with you.'

'No!' She responded so sharply that I was taken aback. 'I'll go on my own.' She looked resolute and angry. I wondered what I had done wrong to bring about this sudden change in her demeanour. What had I done to upset her?

At this point the taxi driver joined in the conversation. Leaning out of the cab window, he grinned at me. 'Don't worry, mate, I'll see she gets home safe and sound.'

By now Eve was inside the cab. Resigned to my fate, I leaned forward into the darkness. 'I'll give you a call,' I said.

She did not answer.

I shut the door and the cab roared off, leaving me in a cloud of exhaust fumes wondering why such a wonderful evening had ended on such a sour note.

nineteen

I slept little that night wondering how I had managed to mar my relationship with Eve. I just hoped that it was the drink that had confused her a little. I thought we were getting on fine. Certainly I'd had a great night but it takes two to tango....

I felt fairly miserable as I drank my first cup of tea of the day but then I brightened at the prospect of my excursion for that afternoon. I was off to a dream factory.

Then I had an idea about Eve. So I decided to put my own acting prowess to the test and adopt the persona of a certain Archie McPherson for a certain phone call.

Denham Studios was some thirty miles out of London. Before the war it had been a thriving film studio owned by Alexander Korda. He had been determined to make it the most modern film studio in Europe but by the late thirties he was in financial difficulties and the money men, in the shape of the Prudential Insurance Company, stepped in and took over. With the outbreak of war, all film production was stopped at nearby Pinewood studios and as a result Denham was swamped with productions. In 1940 it was working around the clock to turn out celluloid fodder to be lapped up by eager audiences desperate to lose themselves in other worlds far away from the reality of war.

The thought of visiting the film studio filled me with excitement. I might be going to interview a suspect in a murder investigation, but he was also Tiger Blake, my childhood film hero. I caught the train to Denham Village with a feeling of suppressed anticipation. I almost forgot the real reason for my journey.

Walking out of the station at Denham I was already conscious that I had left some of the dreariness and destruction of grey London behind. The sky seemed cleaner and the faces of people seemed fresher here. It was as though the shadow of war was not as dark or all-embracing in this semi-rural setting as it was in the damaged metropolis.

I felt a childish thrill as I announced my destination to the ancient cab driver. 'Denham Film Studios please.' Within five minutes I had been dropped off at the gates. The place certainly looked like a factory with its grey blocks of buildings and circular drum-like structures. The ghost of Alexander Korda was in evidence in the large faded lettering that ran down the length of one block stating LONDON FILM PRODUCTIONS. It was strange to think that within its walls fairy tales from all ages were created to be projected in cinemas around the world, allowing anyone with a few shillings or the equivalent to enter the magic escapist world of the cinema.

As I approached the entrance, a little man emerged through the swing doors and scuttled down the steps. My mouth dropped open in recognition. It was the comedian Arthur Askey. Obviously used to such reactions, he gave me a grin, touched his hat and hurried on.

I entered the foyer of Denham Studios through a pair of smoked-glass swing doors and passed into a gently humming beehive. The sound of suppressed activity was all around. Above me running around the whole area was a metal gangway along which many worker bees made their way, some carrying files, boxes, brief cases, while others strolled together in deep muttered converse. Occasionally one or two of them would disappear down a corridor running off from this mezzanine only to be replaced by others emerging from their own warren. It was all very futuristic, unreal, and reminded me of the sets of Korda's version of H.G. Wells' *Things to Come*. Perhaps he had modelled those on Denham, or vice-versa.

A commissionaire in a blue coat with gold braid at his shoulders stepped forward to meet me. Meet me rather than greet me. He was a large man, probably ex-army, ruddy of face and no-nonsense of nature.

'What is your business here, sir?' he said in a mechanical way. There was no real unpleasantness in his delivery, but I could not help detect a vague note of menace in his demeanour. Obviously he was there as the first barrier to prevent any star-struck film fan on a mission to obtain an autograph or catch a glimpse of their favourite star, from entering the building.

'I'm Gus Andrews from *ScreenTime* magazine. I'm here to interview Gordon Moore. I have an appointment with Tristan Williams of Regent Films at two-thirty.'

The blue-coated warrior's attitude altered immediately. His shoulders relaxed and his tight mouth relaxed. 'Just have a word with Sonia at the desk and she'll sort you out.'

Sonia was a busty young woman with half the make-up department on her face. It was obvious that she was hoping to be spotted by some producer or director passing through the foyer who would star her in his latest film.

'How can I help you?' she asked, in a husky mid-Atlantic drawl, her glossy red lips pouting at me as though they had a life of their own.

I told her the same story as I'd told the commissionaire. Her fingers tapped viciously on the intercom system and moments later a sibilant voice emerged from a tiny speaker.

'Yes, what is it?' There was irritation in every word.

'A Mr Gus Andrews from *ScreenTime* has arrived,' the red lips emoted into the microphone.

This information was greeted by a weary sigh. 'I'll be down in a few minutes,' said Tristan before cutting himself off abruptly.

Before Sonia could relay this gem of information to me, I smiled and said, 'I heard.'

'If you'll just take a seat,' she purred, indicating a row of cinema seats across from the desk.

I did as I was bid and sat twiddling my thumbs. After ten minutes Tristan arrived. He was much as I imagined him. A lanky fellow, like me in his late twenties, but unlike me with an unruly mop of long hair and owlish glasses perched on the end of his long hooter. He was dressed in grey flannels and a shapeless rust-coloured jumper and for some reason he had a college scarf around his neck.

'Mr Andrews, sorry to keep you waiting. It's been one of those days.'

I bet you say that to all the boys.

'That's OK,' I said, offering my hand. Surprisingly he gave it a hefty, manly shake.

'Come with me,' he beckoned, leading me up a staircase which led to the mezzanine. I was really going to enter the inner sanctum of filmdom.

He leaned close to me with a confidential air. 'In your line of business you probably realize that stars can be ... temperamental, to say the least. They are under such pressure to perform and be someone they are not that sometimes they can forget to be human. They can have their off days.'

It was his polite way of telling me that film actors can be a pain in the arse.

'So Mr Moore has been a little difficult ...?'

Tristan looked as though he was about to indulge a large bout of indiscretion but manfully he bottled it and just nodded. 'Difficult just about sums it up.'

'He's still going to see me though?'

He shrugged. 'I hope so.'

Tristan led me along a narrow corridor, down a flight of steps and through a door marked Studio H1. We stepped into what looked like an aircraft hangar. It was filled with cameras, lights, boom microphones and all the attendant paraphernalia of film making. I'd seen pictures so I know. There were also several individual sets, one of which appeared to be a prison cell, but the studio seemed deserted.

'This is where they are shooting the new Tiger Blake,' said Tristan, 'but the crew have broken for an early lunch.'

I nodded, trying to appear like a world-weary film journalist to whom all this was old hat rather than the avid film fan I was, an innocent who had wandered into the magic kingdom. As we skirted the perimeter of the building we passed an enormous set with palm trees, sand and a lugubrious camel that was completely occupied in chewing some disgusting strawlike concoction.

'The oasis,' explained Tristan. 'We have a big gun battle to film there later in the week.'

'Oh, have we?'

Tristan nodded. 'Don't want to give the game away but Tiger gets badly injured in that scene.'

This information was imported in a part whisper as though my guide was breaking some confidential rule of his profession by leaking out the information. It came as no surprise to me, however: Tiger Blake always got badly injured at the beginning of the last reel, only to recover miraculously before the closing credits.

At the back of Studio H1 there was a row of low buildings resembling the utilitarian pre-fabricated houses which were springing up all round London to house the bombed homeless. These were smaller but looked tidier and more glamorous. Tristan led me to one of these, which had the name of Gordon Moore painted on the door along with a silver star.

'Mr Moore's dressing-room,' said Tristan, unnecessarily. 'This is where he rests up and checks his lines for the next shoot.'

I nodded.

'Now, if you'll wait here, I'll see if Mr Moore is ready to see you.'

Gingerly he tapped on the door. There was no response. He tapped again, louder this time. And this time there was a response.

'Go away,' bellowed a voice from within.

Tristan raised his eyebrows and gave me a look which said, 'Told you he could be difficult.'

'It's Tristan, Mr Moore. I have Gus Andrews here from

ScreenTime. You remember you agreed he could interview you for his magazine.'

There was a pause and then the door was wrenched open. Tiger Blake stood before me. Well, to be precise, a raddled, paunchy, blotchy-faced Tiger Blake wearing an obvious toupee stood before me. He grinned in a theatrical manner at me. 'Of course, Mr Andrews. Do come into my bothy. I can give you ten minutes.' The grin disappeared as quickly as it came.'

'Thank you,' I said humbly and followed him inside.

'Come back for him in ten minutes,' Moore called to Tristan as he closed the door. It was an instruction, not a request.

The room was cramped, with a make-up mirror, table and chair, a small wardrobe and a large camp-bed. By the bed, on the floor, was a tray containing a large bottle of gin and an empty glass. Moore slumped on the bed and snatched up the glass. It was clear there'd be no drinkies for me.

'So laddo, what d'you want to know, eh? What kind of crap do you want to feed to your readers, eh? Well, I can give you an exclusive if you want.'

I nodded, not wanting to interrupt his flow with words.

'This is my last Tiger Blake movie. I have decided to give up making these bloody films. An actor of my calibre deserves something more, something better.' He took a big slurp of his gin. 'I was RADA trained you know. Did a season at Stratford, too. And where do I end up? Running through cardboard forests and shooting a lot of foreigners.'

He looked at me over the rim of his glass to gauge my reaction to his news. I didn't give him one, but stared steadily back at him.

He pursed his lips, the fire of his anger waning. 'So there you have it. Tiger Blake retires and Gordon Moore shuffles off into oblivion. What else do you need to know?'

'I'd like to know if you killed Pammie Palmer.'

At first I thought he was going to have some kind of heart attack. He gave a sharp, guttural cry as his eyes bulged from their sockets, his face darkened to a deep red and he gripped his glass so tightly his knuckles beamed white.

'Who the fuck are you?' he asked at length.

'That doesn't matter.'

'Oh, but it does. Are you the bastard who's been calling me?'

I shook my head.

'Then who the hell are you? What do you want?'

'I want the truth. Did you kill Pammie?'

Gordon Moore stared at me for some moments. I could not tell whether he was angry or frightened. My guess was that he was both. He poured himself another drink and took a large gulp.

'No, I did not kill her.'

'But you visited her on the night she died. You were a client of hers. You rang her from a call box on Boynton Street, near your club and arranged to ... see her at her flat.'

'How ... how do you know all this?'

'That's not important. If you didn't kill Pammie, you'd better tell me what happened that night.'

'Go to hell!'

'All in good time. But if you are at all interested in saving your neck, I'd advise you to tell me the truth, otherwise you'll have the police knocking on your door and they'll want more than ten minutes of your time, I can promise you that.'

At the mention of the police, the colour began to drain from Moore's mottled face.

'Do you want money?'

I shook my head. 'I just want the truth. Tell me about that night.'

twenty

Gordon Moore's Story

I'd had a terrible day. I received a message to visit my agent
that afternoon. I assumed that it was about those bastards at
Regent Films haggling about my fee for the new Tiger Blake
farrago. They always came up with excuses to try and pay me
a little less than the previous picture, but Bruce Mellor, my
agent, is a shrewd guy and he usually got me a decent deal. So
when I visited his office I had no notion that he was about to
drop a bloody great bombshell. He didn't beat about the bush,
but told it to me straight. Regent weren't haggling about my
fee. They were happy to pay it because I was getting the push.
After this picture they didn't want me any more. I had out-lived
my usefulness. They intended to bring in a younger, more
attractive actor to take my part. Apparently, they were going to
re-vamp the series, make it more appealing to the young or
some such nonsense. In simple terms, I was washed up. You
cannot imagine what that felt like. I was sick to my stomach.
After fifteen years of playing the same stupid part how was
anyone going to take me seriously as an actor ... as a star? It
was as though I was staring into a black abyss.

Bruce muttered his condolences and tried his best to
convince me that this could be a real chance for me to get better,
more lucrative parts. They were empty sentiments – a load of
manure, in fact. I could see it in his eyes. A turning point in my
career, he said. Well, it's that all right. Turning off the main
road up some narrow unmade track heading for oblivion. Of
course, Bruce realized that with my departure from the star's

dressing-room, he was losing out as well. No more healthy percentages from old Tiger Blake.

I escaped the confines of his office and wandered the streets for a while trying to come terms with the horrible truth. But I couldn't. How could I? The Tiger Blake movies and all the perks that went with them had been part of my life for over twelve years. I was in a state of bereavement.

Eventually, I went to my club and as usual tried to drown my sorrows in drink. But on this occasion, alcohol proved ineffective. Instead of leading me into the realms of misty amnesia, it only fuelled my anger and despair. Despite downing several large gins I stayed sober. I remained conscious and painfully aware of my own tragedy. If that sounds dramatic, just put yourself in my position. I was a film star, known all over the world for playing Tiger Blake, hero and tough guy. Always caught the baddie and always got the girl. It was my life, my livelihood and my key to all sorts of privileges. And now that had all been taken away from me. What have I to look forward to now? Bit parts in lousy B pictures and weeks in provincial rep – where I bloody started thirty years ago. What happens to my nice clothes, my big car, my world? I lose it all. Tragedy it is, I assure you. The brutal truth of my situation was too great to be affected by drink. But I needed some solace, something to cushion me against the pain of that great big dagger that had been stuck in my back, stuck there by those bastards at Regent Films. I needed love and tenderness. I needed passion. Well, I knew I wouldn't get that at home. You won't have met Mrs Moore, Sandra, have you? She could give the ice maiden a few lessons in frostiness.

Yes, I needed a woman. It wasn't the first time, of course. I can't remember the last occasion I made love to my wife. Well, with Sandra it wasn't so much making love as entering enemy territory. Our marriage hasn't been a marriage of any sort for years. We live separate lives. She is content. She doesn't want anyone else: she has herself.

However, I am different. I am not ashamed to say that I have sought out women to satisfy my need over the years. Sought them out regularly, if you want to know. Some have been willing young actresses, hoping that by letting me bed them it would increase their chances of stardom. Silly cows. And then, more recently, I've paid for services rendered. As I did with Pammie. But she was special. Although there was always a financial transaction at the end of the process, the love-making was tender, exciting. It was as though she cared about you. Not like some of the ten-bob hags round Soho who start filing their nails while you're on the job, eyes as vacant as an empty coffin. And just as comforting. I really believe that Pammie cared a little about me.

Anyway, I rang her up that night. Yes, I did use the phone box on Boynton Street. I didn't want any of the nosy sods at the Corona to hear me. I didn't care a toss about them knowing I was calling a woman – I wouldn't be the only one – I just didn't want them to know about my destiny with the scrapheap. Not just yet anyway. I couldn't bear those furtive looks of sympathy – or worse still those knowing nods of the 'not before time' variety.

I explained my problem to Pammie. She was very sympathetic and invited me round. She said she had a friend already booked in at nine – she always called her clients friends – but she'd make an exception and see me at eleven. Just to hear her voice made me feel better. I went back to the club to wait. I avoided any more alcohol. I didn't want to be incapable when I got to Pammie's. I needed to prove to myself that I could still be a man in one department even if I wasn't going to be a film star much longer. I had a light dinner and drank copious cups of coffee.

I walked round to Pammie's flat feeling strangely numb inside. The pain and sadness had subsided and I was looking forward to an hour of love-making and that was all. It was as though my mind couldn't go beyond that. I couldn't see further than midnight.

When I got to the flat I was surprised to find the door slightly ajar. I knew she would be expecting me, but she usually checked all her visitors through the spyglass in the door before letting them in. I entered and called out her name. There was no response. All the lights were on and the radiogram in the sitting-room was playing some dance band programme. I looked in all the rooms, leaving the bedroom until last. It was as though I knew that's where I would find her.

I went in and there she was – lying on the bed with a knife stuck in her chest. She was dressed in a long white negligee and it glistened where the blood had seeped through the material. At first I couldn't believe what I saw. It was as though I had stepped into one of my own films. This was a stunt double with fake blood. Anytime now someone would call, 'Cut!' But they didn't. The girl did not get up, give me a smile and go for a fag. She just lay there. In this scene she really was dead.

I stood looking at her for some time, trying to take it all in. Eventually, I felt for her pulse, knowing there wouldn't be one. I gazed down at her. She still looked beautiful. Her mouth was open slightly and her eyes were wide with terror. In some strange way it was erotic. I don't know why – I can't even explain it now – but I put out my hand and touched the blood. It was cold and sticky and adhered to my fingers like strawberry jam. It was then that I started crying. All the personal pain and hurt that I'd felt through the day somehow seemed connected with the brutal death of this beautiful young woman and it was too much for me. I'm not ashamed that I sobbed uncontrollably.

I left the flat still in some state of distress. My mind had shut down. I didn't think about calling the police. What could they do? Couldn't bring her back to life, that's for certain. Perhaps some spark of self preservation was still working for me. Being involved with the police certainly would be heaping more coals upon my head. Not only losing my job as Tiger Blake, but found in the flat of a murdered prostitute. That certainly would put the tin hat on my career.

I remember little of what I did next until I arrived home. I know I still had some blood on my hands. I had a bath and scrubbed myself down as though I was expunging the horrors of the whole day. Of course Sandra was already asleep. We don't even share the same bedroom any more so I was safe from questions. For the first time in years I went to bed that night stone cold sober.

That's the truth.

twenty-one

When Gordon Moore had finished telling me his story, he stared at his feet for some moments collecting his thoughts. I let him. It was a convincing tale but he was an actor and used to presenting made up events as the truth. How good an actor was he? It had seemed to me that he had almost been relieved to tell someone, treating me as a father confessor, but was it real or a performance?

I pulled out a pack of cigarettes from my pocket and offered him one.

'Thanks,' he said quietly. All the previous bombast had evaporated or at least had been put on the back burner for a while. Was this all part of the act as well? As I held out a match and lit his cigarette I noticed that his eyes were moist. If this was a performance it was better than any he had given in a dozen Tiger Blake movies.

'So now I've told you what I know about Pammie's death, shouldn't you tell me who the hell you are?'

I passed him one of my cards.

'A private detective.' He said it as though he had just noticed some dog dirt on his shoe.

'I have been employed by Pammie's parents to find the murderer.'

'I thought the police had done that already. It was that pimp, her boyfriend, Fraser.'

'You don't want to believe all you read in the newspapers, Mr Moore. I would have thought you'd know that.'

'Maybe.' He threw his head back and blew out a cloud of white smoke which obscured his face for a moment. The old arrogance was gradually surfacing again. 'So what are going to do about what I've told you?'

'Store it up here' – I tapped my forehead – 'until I've finished my enquiries.'

'I see. Do you believe me?'

I didn't reply, partly because I wasn't sure.

'I didn't kill Pammie. What motive could I possibly have?'

'I don't know. I've more to find out yet. For example, when I first mentioned Pammie's murder, you asked if I was "the bastard who's been calling me".'

Moore nodded. 'I've had a couple of calls from some odd ball who says things.'

'Like what?'

'That I killed her ... stabbed her to death!'

'Yes?'

'... And he's going to see that justice is done.'

'What do you think he means by that?'

'You're the detective! What the hell do you think he means? He's just a crank.'

'Maybe, but cranks can be dangerous and he must know you visited Pammie on the night of her death.'

Moore's eyes flickered nervously. 'Yes,' he said slowly. Obviously this thought had not struck him before.

'And you've no idea whatsoever who the caller is?'

'Not a clue.'

At this point our conversation was interrupted by a tap at the door and Tristan's head popped into view. 'You all through?'

'You could say that,' muttered Gordon Moore, pouring himself a large gin.

While I travelled back to London, I re-ran Gordon Moore's story in my own personal mind cinema. While all the details rang true, it would have been easy for him just to change the details of what happened after he reached Pammie's flat. Perhaps he was drunk and they had a row. In the mood he was in he could have done anything. Anything ... like sticking a knife in her chest.

When he realized the full horror of what he had done, that's when the guilt and remorse set in and the tears. And we were back to the script again.

Maybe.

And then there were the phone calls. Was he concocting these to distance himself from the crime? Inventing threatening messages to throw me off the scent? I thought not. His response was too immediate, too natural to be contrived. And so, that must mean somewhere out there was another person looking into the death of Pammie Palmer. Someone with a dangerous mission.

Once back in the city I made my way to Charing Cross Hospital. There I received the good news that Peter had regained consciousness and was sitting up and taking solids. Apparently he'd scoffed down a hearty breakfast and had been chatting to the nurses. I was envious. Luckily I had encountered the sister who had been on duty when I'd been to see Peter so there was no problem about me going in to see the boy.

When I asked if I could have a chat with him alone, the sister gave me a wary eye but there was a twinkle in it. She told me that I had 'just five minutes' and I was 'not to weary the mite'.

Peter was reading a copy of *The Beano* when I went in. He looked up and at first he gave me an instinctive smile of recognition but then his features clouded, uncertain how he should regard me. I suppose I still represented a figure of authority, someone who could take him back to from where he had escaped.

'Hello there, Peter. Remember me? Johnny, the Spam man.'

He smiled again despite his unease.

I pointed at the comic. 'What's Big Eggo up to this week?'

'Oh, he's trying to get his football back from his neighbour's garden but she catches him and throws a tub of water over him,' he said enthusiastically, happy to share the information.

I chuckled. 'Let me see.' He passed over the garishly coloured comic and I skimmed the simple drawings illustrating the adventures of Big Eggo, the ludicrous humanized ostrich who featured on the front page of *The Beano*. I pretended to follow the plot and chuckled again before handing the comic back. 'He always gets it wrong, does Big Eggo. I'll bring you some more comics when I come again.'

'One of the nurses got me this one,' he said softly, and then looked away shyly. I suspected that he was steeling himself for the moment when I started asking him awkward questions about his home and his mother and father.

'I'll see if I can find you a *Tiger Blake Adventure Comic*. I know you like him.'

At first Peter's eye lit up with pleasure at the thought of a Tiger Blake comic and again they darkened with uncertainty.

'Oh,' I said, 'have you gone off old Tiger? Is that since you saw him?' It was an outrageous prompt but I had to take the risk.

Peter looked at me sharply and his tiny frame stiffened. He shook his head. 'I saw ... I saw him crying ... like a sissy.'

I shook my head sadly. 'Crikey, that's not like old Tiger.'

'No. He never does it in the pictures. He's tough and brave and ...'

'Certainly is. Did you see the way he knocked those Germans about in *The Lost City*?'

Peter grinned. His whole pale, shiny face lit up with pleasure. 'Yes, when he hit that fat Nazi over the head with that thing and he fell through the window into the river. That was great.'

I laughed along with him. 'So are you sure this chap you saw crying really was Tiger Blake?'

Peter sat forward in bed, nodding his head vigorously 'Oh, yes, I'm positive it was him.'

'Where was this?'

'Well, it was when I was trying to get into the park....' He hesitated, realizing where I had led him.

'Regent's Park?' I asked gently.

He gave me a nod.

'Oh, don't you worry about all that. I know where you hid ... and all those things. That doesn't matter now. I'm not here to tell you off or anything. I'm more interested in Tiger Blake. Can't believe he was crying.'

'Oh, but he was. I was across the street from him. I was just about to climb over the railings when I heard him. I thought it was a lady at first – the noise I mean 'cos it was like my ... like a lady's kind of crying. Y'know.' He gave a high-pitched whimpering sound as a demonstration.

'Yes, I know,' I said conspiratorially.

'Well, I looked and saw it was a bloke. As he walked along, he was sort of staring at his hands. It was fairly dark 'cos it was the blackout but the moon sort of lit him up.'

'Why was he looking at his hands?'

'Well, they seemed to be covered in some dark stuff. Don't know what it was.... It could have been mud I suppose. Anyway, then he looks up, sort of puts his head back....' Peter demonstrated once again. 'And I saw him quite clearly. The moon shone down right on his face. No doubt. I'd know Tiger Blake anywhere. And he was crying. His face was wet and he kept making that funny squeaky sound.'

'Well, I'll be blowed. What a surprise.'

'Yeah. I don't think I like him any more. You're not supposed to cry if you're a man are you? And a Special Agent as well.'

'Well, I suppose he might have been pretending. He could have been on a case and he had to pretend he was crying, upset over something, to convince the enemy he was a softy.'

'To fool them? Like he did in *Tiger Blake and the Castle of Death*?'

'That's it.'

Peter pursed his lips. 'I never thought of that.'

'Bet that's the answer.'

Peter nodded thoughtfully. 'I expect you're right.'

'You didn't see anyone else about at the time, did you? Someone in the shadows?'

Peter shook his head. 'No. There was no one else.'

'Well', I said cheerfully, 'I'm glad we've got that sorted out. I'd hate to think that good old Tiger was a softy.'

'Me too,' Peter grinned at me.

'Anyway, how are you feeling?'

'OK, I guess.'

'Are they feeding you any better than I did?'

Peter giggled. 'I had two whole boiled eggs this morning with some soldiers.'

'Wow, lucky you.'

At this point the sister made an appearance. 'You two been having a nice chat?'

'Yes,' I said, 'sorting one or two things out.'

'Really?' She smiled that severe smile that nurses in authority seemed to manage with great aplomb. 'Well, it's nearly time for Master Peter's medicine and then he needs a good rest, so I'll have to ask you to go now, Mr Hawke.'

'Certainly, Sister.' I gave an exaggerated bow. Peter grinned at my clowning. 'I'll be back tomorrow with some comics,' I told him.

As I headed for the door, I took the sister to one side. 'Could I have a word with you outside before I go?'

She nodded. 'I'll just give the patient his medicine and I'll be with you in a moment.'

'What's going to happen to Peter?' I asked when the sister joined me in the corridor.

She gave a heavy sigh. 'Well, he maintains that his mum and dad are dead and that's about as much as we can get out of him. He doesn't fit any of the missing children's files the police have, so he's a bit of a mystery. He's obviously a distressed little boy. He wets the bed.' She sighed again. 'I'm afraid when he's well enough to leave here he'll be taken into an orphanage if only as a temporary measure while further investigations are carried out. But I don't hold out much hope that anything will be found out. There's hundreds of lads and lassies in a similar situation and there's not enough manpower to cope with the situation.'

My stomach lurched at the mention of orphanage. The contemplation of such bleak institutions chilled me to the marrow as though I'd been dipped in an ice-cold pond. I knew all about orphanages. I was an old campaigner. I had the bruises and the traumas to prove it.

For a moment I had a vision of a younger me staring out of the window of the cramped dormitory at Moorfield towards the high wall with the broken glass cemented into the top of it. The glass glinted in the moonlight like vicious diamonds. I was wondering what the world beyond the grim confines could offer me. Certainly something better than the harsh regime of Moorfield, I was sure. I felt a hand pull at my pyjama jacket as Paul, my brother, attempted to guide me back to my bed. 'If you're caught out here, you'll be for it, Johnny,' he whispered in my ear. Ever the guardian angel was Paul. With some effort he pulled me away from my dreams and back to the cold hard bed with its rough blanket.

Moorfield the home for orphaned boys. Home? Prison, more like.

'Are you all right?' the sister asked.

'Yes, I suppose so,' I said, faking a smile and shaking off the ghosts of my past. 'I have some personal experience of orphanages. They are not exactly the institutions that make for a happy childhood.'

'But without them where we would be? Especially now there are so many poor blighters who have lost their parents in this bloody war.'

'Bloody war, indeed. Look, Sister, I want to help as much as I can with this boy, Peter. Somehow I feel responsible for him. Don't let them take him away before you let me know.' Quickly, I scribbled my telephone number on a piece of paper. I could have given her one of my cards but I didn't want her to know that I was a detective. That fact might change her whole opinion of me. It usually did.

'I'll make sure, Mr Hawke,' she said, smiling as she secreted the paper under the fold of her stiff uniform. 'It won't be for a few days yet. The little mite is still quite weak.'

'Thank you. And call me Johnny, please.'

She blushed a little. 'I'm Sister McAndrew ... Susan.'

I leaned forward and gave her a kiss on the cheek and she blushed even further. 'That's enough of that,' she said gently, 'or I'll think you're only here for ulterior motives.'

'Absolutely.'

We both laughed and took pleasure in the moment, realizing that we were snatching a gentle, whimsical interval from the ragged, grey, dispiriting play of life.

'I'll be back to see Peter tomorrow.' I gave her a wave and strolled down the bleak corridor with something approaching a warm feeling in my heart.

twenty-two

Two Telephone Calls
(1)

Sandra Moore was bored. She was often bored. There was little in life to entertain her except buying smart clothes, attending nice parties and dining in expensive restaurants. Since this awful war had started with its wretched rationing, these activities had been severely restricted. What was worse, some of her friends had deserted her, left London for the country to escape the bombing. She would have loved to go with them. She saw their desertion not as an act of cowardice and self-preservation but one of eminent sense and rationality. Oh to be holed up in some comfortable 'funk hole' hotel with them. But Gordon was tied to the capital with his job, one which gave him an income with which he was able to provide her with all the civilized comforts she required, indeed insisted upon, to make her life bearable.

Sandra had one great love in her life – herself. She had forsaken all other loves but herself. Gordon, whom she had relegated to the periphery of her existence, was glimpsed only as a provider. If a horse could have earned the same amount of money as Gordon – preferably more – it would have done for her just as well. Better, actually, because a horse could be stabled outside the house.

These idle thoughts strolled through Sandra's mind as she puffed on her third cigarette of the morning. Stubbing it out half smoked, she moved to the mirror and checked her make-up. It was perfect. She forced a broad unnatural smile at herself to check the laugh lines. Not bad. She was indeed a handsome, some would say pretty woman who belied her forty-three years. Or at least she thought so.

The shrill ring of the telephone broke in upon this self-congratulatory reverie. She pursed her lips. Who could this be? Was it a summons for lunch by an old friend in town for the day or some even more exciting prospect? She hoped so.

Sandra moved elegantly to the telephone table in the hall. She did not rush. She had no intention of creating the impression that she was eager for the call – although she was. She was eager for anything that would lift her out of the mind-numbing ennui in which she was immersed.

'Sandra Moore,' she purred into the receiver.

'Ah', said the voice at the other end, 'the wife of the whore murderer.'

This certainly wasn't the call Sandra was hoping for. She was about to put the telephone down when the caller spoke again. 'Don't go, Sandra, I have important information to impart to you.'

'Who is this?'

'A friend.'

'Then identify yourself.' For one fleeting moment she wondered if it really was one of Gordon's cronies making this tasteless call.

'Not at the moment, Sandra,' came the hoarse and muffled voice again. 'But let me give you the reason for calling you. I just wanted to put you in the picture about your husband and Pammie Palmer.'

'Pammie who?'

'Don't you read the newspapers, Sandra? Pammie Palmer, the whore who got herself killed in her flat in Regent's Park mansions. Did you know that your husband was one of her customers, eh?'

Sandra was well aware that Gordon sought sexual favours elsewhere and she didn't care as long as he didn't seek them with her and he kept his sordid flings away from the domestic arena.

'Do you have a point? If not I shall put the phone down.'

'Oh, I have a point, Sandra. Very sharp and piercing is my point. Not only was your film star husband a client of the Palmer trollop but he also murdered her. He stuck a knife in her chest.'

Sandra gave a little gasp of disgust.

'Now, Sandra, I don't expect you to take my word for it. I want you to ask your husband about it. Don't be bashful. Just ask him outright. "Why did you kill the Palmer whore?" I'm sure his reaction will be very interesting. Do try it out. I shall ring you again to find out what he said. Goodbye, Sandra.'

With that the line went dead.

(2)

Gordon Moore was back in his dressing-room. It was late afternoon and he had struggled through the difficult inter-rogation scene – so much expository dialogue – and was relieved to be away from the cameras. Since the humiliating news of his sacking he hated appearing in front of the cameras more than ever. He wasn't sure how many people knew this was to be his last Tiger Blake picture but he was aware it wouldn't be long before the news leaked out and then there'd be a lot of sniggering and grinning behind his back on the studio floor. He had never gone out of his way to ingratiate himself with co-stars or the technicians. They would be delighted at his downfall.

He felt sure that Norman Lee, the director, would have been informed about his dismissal, which would please the old bastard immensely. Then a thought struck him as he uncorked the gin bottle. If the bosses of Regent Films wanted to re-vamp the Tiger Blake series, probably they would be getting rid of Lee too. Moore grinned for the first time that day. He hoped they sent him packing back to Hollywood and landed him with directing The Three Stooges – the Californian equivalent of the salt mines. Frankly, Lee's directorial techniques had not developed since the day of the silents. It's a wonder he didn't bring a megaphone on to the set. Moore warmed to the image of Norman Lee tearing his hair out as Larry, Mo and Curly ignored his directorial instructions.

'Serve the bastard right,' he observed to his reflection in the make-up mirror before downing a tumbler of gin. It burned his throat and caused him to cough a little but he kept smiling. Cheered by the thought of Lee also getting the chop, he began the tedious process of taking off his make-up. He was reluctant to remove the toupee. He had resisted having to wear one at first but now he liked it. It really did make him look younger. Perhaps he ought to investigate the use of one in real life, particularly as in a few months he'd be scrabbling around for parts. He needed to retain the image of himself as he appeared on the screen.

The phone rang. Without thinking, he snatched it up. It was Tristan. 'Sorry to bother you, Mr Moore, but I've got another urgent call from Pammie Palmer's office. They said you would be expecting it. Shall I put it through?'

The warm glow that had been starting to suffuse his body, helping him to relax, vanished at the mention of Pammie's name.

'Yes. Put it through,' he said mechanically. What fresh hell was this?

At first there was a hissing silence on the line and then a voice spoke. It was the same voice as last time.

'Mr Moore?'

'What do you want?'

'I want nothing, Mr Moore. The purpose of this call is to provide you with information.' The tone was cold, precise but with an underlying threat in the delivery.

'Well, go on then. Get it off your chest,' snapped Moore. He had gone so far down the road of despair that he was becoming immune to new terrors.

'I thought you should know that I felt it my duty to inform your wife that you are a whore murderer—'

'My wife!'

'Yes, Sandra Moore. She seemed quite shocked at the news.'

'You bastard.'

'Such profanity. Still what can one expect from a whore murderer?'

'I haven't murdered anyone. I don't know who you are and why you have got this twisted notion into your head. But I am innocent. I did not kill anyone. So you can go to the Devil.'

'On the contrary, Mr Moore, it is you who will be going to the Devil – and quite soon.'

'What on earth do you mean?'

'Murder is a sin which is punishable by death. You have but a little time to place your affairs in order. Are you familiar with Deuteronomy, chapter 19, verse 21?'

Gordon Moore was now convinced he had a madman on the line and was about to put the receiver back on its cradle when the voice came again.

'However, you are probably familiar with the phrase found at this part of the scriptures: "an eye for eye, a tooth for a tooth". In simple translation, it means a life for a life. I hope you appreciate the implication of this. I am going you kill you, Mr Moore. And soon. Goodbye.'

The line went dead and Gordon Moore found himself looking at his own horrified features staring back at him from the make-up mirror.

twenty-three

As I emerged from the hospital, I was greeted by a fine but insidious mist of rain. Pulling up my collar, I headed for home. I decided to walk and let my mind do some thinking. To be honest my head ached with ideas and thoughts that crowded the narrow passageways of my throbbing brain. I had acquired a lot of information, but yet I didn't seem to be getting any nearer to pointing the finger at Pammie's killer.

As I walked, I began to play the Agatha Christie game where you assemble all the known suspects in the library and assess their suitability for the role of murderer.

To begin with, there was Sam Fraser, boyfriend, pimp and the most obvious suspect, now languishing in a cell awaiting a foregone conclusion of a trial, courtesy of Inspector Knight. Of course, as a little voice whispered to me, the most obvious suspect is often the guilty one – that is why they're the most obvious suspect. Life – and certainly crime – is rarely as complicated or convoluted as it is in the movies. But another voice told me that he just wasn't the guy. I had no facts to back up this instinct, just my very fallible judgement of character.

Then there was the oily Leo Epstein. There was more to this fellow than met my eye. Thanks to Eve, I knew that his story about his one night of misjudged passion with Pammie was just the tip of the iceberg. So he was a liar. But then he was a solicitor and that's what they do for a living. Like so many men, it seemed, Epstein had become besotted by the girl. But if that was the case, why on earth would he want to kill her? Did she hold some threat over him – was she blackmailing him perhaps? Or was he devastated when he found out that she gave her favours to other men for a fee?

The third occupant of my imaginary library was our film star, Gordon Moore. I just wasn't sure about him at all. He had been in Pammie's flat the night she was killed and Peter's sighting of him confirmed that Moore had left with blood on his hands and in a distressed state. But was he distressed because he had found the body or because he had killed someone? He seemed to have so many demons in his life. Did he lash out at the thing that he treasured the most: a whore who made him feel loved?

Despite this promising cast, I could not help thinking that there was another shadowy figure in my library whose features I couldn't see and whose identity was as yet a closed book to me – quite appropriate for a library I suppose. Could this be the individual who had clobbered me on the back of the head? Was he Moore's phantom caller?

I just didn't know. Not yet, I didn't.

But I would.

I closed the library door and my thoughts turned to Eve. The delightful, the delovely, the enigmatic Eve. I smiled as I did so. I really liked her and I thought she liked me, or at least she was intrigued by me, which was a start. However, I was puzzled by her strange behaviour at the end of the previous evening when I had suggested that I see her home. We'd had a good night together and things had gone swimmingly until it was time to go home. Then she had grown decidedly frosty as though I had made improper advances. Was it really something that I had done or said that made her act that way or was she covering up, trying to hide the truth from me? That's all I needed: another mystery.

As I approached Hawke Towers I was weary and longed for a cup of tea. When I got back to my office, it was already growing dark and a purple dusk was wrapping itself around the city. I found that I had a visitor waiting on my doorstep. It was Mr Palfrey. His hair was plastered down by the rain and his glasses were spotted with moisture.

'I hope you haven't been here long,' I said, opening up.

He shook his head.

I threw off my hat and raincoat and switched on the lights. 'Would you care for a cup of tea? You look rather damp.'

He shook his head again. 'No thank you, Mr Hawke. I am here purely on a matter of business.'

'OK,' I said, sitting on the edge of my desk, dismayed that I'd have to wait for my tea. 'I expect you want an update on how my investigations are going.'

Palfrey shook his head vigorously. 'You are wrong in your expectations, Mr Hawke. I am here for a quite different reason.'

'Oh?'

'I am here to ask you to cease your investigations into Pamela's murder. When my wife and I engaged you it was for the purpose of discovering the whereabouts of our daughter. That, in a sense, in a terrible sense, has now been achieved and although we appreciate your concerns about her death we really do not want you to carry on ... stirring things up, prolonging our pain. I don't think my wife can take much more. The police have their man and we are satisfied with their findings. You must, you must ... stop it.'

He spoke with a passionate nervous urgency and delivered his thoughts as though he had been rehearsing them for some time. I wondered how much his wife agreed with him.

'What are you frightened of, Mr Palfrey?'

'Frightened?' This seemed to throw him at first. He was off the script now. Then with an arching of his shoulders, he rallied to the challenge of an impromptu response. 'I am not frightened of anything and neither is my wife. What have we cause to be frightened of anything any more? Our worst nightmare has come true. We have lost our daughter, our little girl, on whom we lavished a great deal of love and affection. Not only have we lost her but in doing so we learned that she cared nothing for us. We were not worth a second thought. We also discovered that she was a prostitute, selling her body for sex. She had become another person with another name and another morality. She had effectively erased us from her life. It is as though we never had a child. So tell me, Mr Hawke, what is there left to be frightened about? We just want it to stop. We don't care who killed Pamela. It won't alter facts. She's dead and she is no longer our daughter.'

His face was suffused with anger and pain. I suppose I should have felt sorry for him but in his tunnel vision of the events he was denying playing any part in the fate of his daughter. I knew this to be wrong.

'I can understand how you feel, but as a detective I have to follow my instincts, too. A murder has been committed and it is my belief that the police have arrested the wrong man. I cannot let the matter lie.'

'That is your business not ours. I know that I cannot prevent you from carrying out your investigations. However, I had hoped that you might do so out of consideration for us....'

'I can't, out of consideration for a murdered girl – your daughter. Whatever she was in life, she didn't deserve to be murdered.'

'Didn't she? Well, whatever you do, we want no further contact with you, Mr Hawke. My wife and I are adamant about this. You are to leave us alone.' He withdrew an envelope from his coat pocket and threw it on to my desk. 'There's a further twenty pounds in there to cover your fees and expenses for the last few days. It is our last payment to you. We are dispensing with your services forthwith.'

I picked up the envelope and held it out to Palfrey. 'Really, there's no need—'

'For God's sake, take it,' he bellowed, jumping to his feet. 'We don't want to be beholden to anyone. It's our way of ending our sordid little arrangement. To draw the line under something that has blighted our lives.'

Palfrey's behaviour could have been comic were it not for the unnerving fanatical gleam in his eyes and the bitterness that shook his frame. His whole demeanour was one of unpredictable anger.

I flapped the envelope before his face. 'If that's the way you want it ...' I said.

'It is. Now it's time I got back to my wife.' He rose stiffly and without another word he left.

I sat for some time staring into middle distance. I had lost clients before but not like this. The Palfreys' lives had been ruined by the discovery that their daughter was not the simple, plain girl they had believed her to be – had, in fact, tried to make her. I sensed from our first encounter that Mr Palfrey had wanted to control Pamela, to create in his eyes the ideal girl according to his standards. Any normal daughter would have rebelled against such strictures. It may well be that part of the anger he exhibited was the result of the guilt he felt. And then again, maybe not.

Well, I shrugged my weary shoulders, clients or not I still had a case to solve.

I wandered over to the gas ring and put the kettle on.

After two cups of Typhoo, three Craven As and a further ponder, I made a telephone call.

A tired voice at the other end recited the number.

'Mrs Palfrey?'

'Yes.' The voice was hesitant.

'John Hawke here.'

'Oh, sorry Mr Hawke, I didn't recognize your voice.'

'That's all right. I've just had a visit from your husband. He's asked me to drop my investigations into Pamela's death.'

There was a pause and then, 'Yes, I thought he would. He can't bear it any longer, you see. He feels so hurt by the whole affair. He is so used to being in charge of things, of his life, that he cannot cope when events go beyond his control. He feels lost, disorientated. He thinks that if he cuts himself off from everything, he'll be able to manage....'

'Pretend it never happened.'

'Yes, I suppose that's it. In one sense you can't blame him. He refuses to talk about Pamela. He denies her existence. In fact he's all but stopped talking to me.'

'And what about you, Mrs Palfrey? How are you coping?'

'As I always have. Stoically, I suppose you might say. Taking each day as it comes. I have a greater degree of acceptance of the cruelty of life than my husband. I was her mother. I can't forget or deny that. Whatever our children do, they are still ours. I grieve as any mother would.'

'Wouldn't the grieving be easier if you knew who was responsible for your daughter's death?'

'I'm not sure that it matters any more. Dead or alive we have lost our Pamela. In truth we lost her before she left home. You might find this difficult to understand, but having found out all about our daughter's ... activities, I believe she is better off dead.'

I really did not know how to respond to that statement. It was as though the woman had brutally severed all her maternal instincts.

'Is it your desire that I should give up my investigations?'

'I think it would be for the best.'

'But it may result in the wrong man being punished.'

'Wrong people are punished all the time. My husband and I are being punished now, just for being loving parents. I have no wish to guide your conscience, Mr Hawke. Please follow your own beliefs and desires if you must, but do not involve us. To be honest, I never wanted to come to you in the first place. My husband is right. We need to be left alone. Goodbye, Mr Hawke.'

The phone went dead.

And so ... follow my own conscience ... and my instincts I must.

twenty-four

Unlike her husband, Sandra Moore did not drink very much. She watched her weight scrupulously and was conscious of the effect that alcohol could have on the smoothness of the skin, the thickness of the waist and the whites of the eyes. But after receiving the telephone call, she had made an exception and downed two large sherries in quick succession. She hoped the drinks would help her relax and allow her to think. She had to decide what to do.

Sandra knew that if her wretched husband had got himself involved with a whore and had murdered her, she had to distance herself from him as far as possible, while retaining as much dignity and money as she could muster. Of course, it wasn't certain that Gordon had committed murder. It was a crank call after all. However, there was no smoke without fire and if it was true, she was in great danger of being dragged down with him. She had seen Gordon drunk and angry and in this state she believed that he was quite capable of killing someone.

Another sherry convinced her that Gordon was as guilty as hell.

She really could not stay put and wait for the truth to come out. The role of the loyal wife was not in her repertoire. She had to act now. There really wasn't a moment to lose. She was pleased she had made that decision. The sherry was working. However the next problem was … what exactly should she do? Luckily, she told herself, she didn't love the bastard. She had no feelings for him whatsoever; in fact she wouldn't care if she never saw him again. Indeed, that would be a welcome outcome. She had only herself to think about. Her instinct was to pack her things, empty their joint back account and escape to Geraldine's in the Cotswolds until the whole ghastly business was over. It would be a pity to leave this lovely flat over which she had lavished much care and attention – the furnishings were exquisite – but she could return to it when it was all over. When Gordon Moore was dangling from a rope.

She suddenly felt the stirrings of anger in her frigid heart. It's a pity he wasn't dead already, she thought. That would save a lot of trouble. Sandra's jaw muscles tightened as the image of her stupid husband flashed into her mind. Whatever happened, she was bound to be affected by the scandal. Damn him! He couldn't even kill a tart without getting caught.

She stood up, smoothed down her skirt and headed for the bedroom to pack.

Parker, the porter at the Corona Club had a struggle helping Gordon Moore on with his overcoat. The actor was more drunk than usual and making no attempt to be a willing participant in the exercise. He'd been alone in the dining-room for most of the evening, eating little but drinking copiously. He was on a morbid mission to blot out the world. When it came time for him to leave, it was as though the world was trying to blot *him* out. Everything was in soft double focus and his limbs had lost their firmness and adopted a rubbery quality.

It was clear even to his befuddled brain that he'd never make it into his overcoat without some assistance. Parker, who had worked at the Corona Club long enough to be telepathic about such situations, came to his rescue. What followed was like a wrestling match in slow motion in which the coat adopted the persona of a third combatant. After a great deal of huffing and puffing along with a series of inarticulate grunts from both men, the task was completed and Moore leaned against the porter somewhat out of breath.

'Are you all right, sir?' asked Parker with genuine concern.

Moore gave a grunt, which was intended to be a laugh. 'Shall

I tell you a little secret, Parker, my friend? I am not all right and I don't think I'll ever be all right again.'

'Oh, don't say that, sir. Every cloud, y'know.'

Moore gave another laughing grunt. 'Every cloud is filled with fucking rain and I got no umbrella any more.'

Parker decided there was no future in following this particular strand of conversation. 'Shall I call you a cab, Mr Moore?'

'No thanks. I'll walk a while. I need some fresh air. Good night, old boy.' Moore pulled himself away from Parker's support and made his way unsteadily to the door. A passing member gave him a wide berth in case he was involved in a collision and flashed Parker an eye-rolling look. The porter responded with an indulgent smile.

Once outside the club, the cold air assailed Moore's senses and he stumbled down the steps and, reaching the bottom, he fell sideways on to the damp pavement. He sprawled lengthways close to the gutter.

'Christ,' he hissed, as pain shot up his arm. There was no one about and he lay there for some moments before he made a great effort to get to his feet. It was an operation which was conducted in stages. He paused after each one while his head stopped swimming. Once he was upright he wriggled the fingers of his right hand. They ached but it seemed that there was no permanent damage. His arm throbbed, too, but he knew that it wasn't broken. He took a deep breath and tried to shake the fog of alcohol from his brain. There was little dispersal.

For some moments he stood, a hunched figure seemingly unable to move. In fact he found some comfort in his immobility, a state in which neither physical nor mental effort was required. Eventually, he heard voices across the street: a man and a woman's. They were chatting cheerily. Good friends or lovers even, on their way home. Their presence prompted Moore to adopt as normal a pose as possible and he began to walk slowly and carefully down the street. His progress was slow but at least it was progress. By the time he had reached the end of the street, his two companions had disappeared into the night, only their voices, now distant echoes in the darkness, disturbed the silence.

He breathed deeply allowing the chill air to invade his lungs, hoping it would brighten his senses. He decided that he would walk a little further, in the direction of Hanley Street where, with a bit of luck, he would be able to pick up a taxi. And then home, bed and welcome oblivion.

With as much determination and energy as he could muster, he set forth. He was desperate for a cigarette but he knew that in his condition extracting the packet and matches from inside his jacket and lighting the bloody thing was beyond his capabilities at present. The co-ordination just wasn't there. It was taking him all his concentration to put one foot in front of the other. For the moment he would have to content himself with sucking in the night air.

As he walked – shuffled would be a more accurate description – he became conscious of another sound: that of footsteps behind him. They were indistinct at first but they grew louder as though they were getting nearer and then they slowed down. God, he hoped it wasn't an ARP Warden 'doing his duty'. Pedantic sods they were. He could find himself in some cop shop for being drunk and incapable in a blackout.

With some effort he stopped and turned around. Sure enough there was a dark figure standing a few yards away watching him. Because of the darkness and his own blurred vision he really couldn't make out any features.

'Good evening,' said Moore, his voice thick and slurred.

The figure stepped a little closer. 'Gordon Moore?' The voice was muffled and strange.

'Why, yes,' replied the actor with some surprise. His brain did not register the danger.

'Gordon Moore, the whore killer?'

Before Moore could assimilate the implication of this statement, the figure stepped forward and thrust a long blade with great force into his stomach, withdrew it and stabbed him again.

Moore gave a gargling cry and pulled back, eyes wide with shock as the pain overwhelmed all other sensations. He clutched his stomach and to his horror he saw a dark liquid streaming through his hands and splashing on the pavement.

He was bereft of words and was only able to express his fear and hurt by a series of horrified grunts. As he staggered backwards, his assailant advanced upon him and stabbed him savagely once more. The blade cut deeply, creating a third and fatal wound.

This time Moore crashed backwards on to the pavement. He was now only capable of inarticulate croaks of pain as life began to ebb away. He glimpsed the dark avenger turn away and slip back into the shadows. It was the last thing he saw, for then the eternal blackness which comes to us all in time wrapped itself around the prone body of Gordon Moore. Another corpse in the dark forest of the night.

Within seconds Tiger Blake was dead.

twenty-five

The next morning I was up with the lark. Well, to be honest I think the lark was still in the bathroom carrying out its ablutions by the time I was chugging along in a tube to Warwick Avenue, Maida Vale. I was engaged on a little investigation of my own which wasn't directly related to the Pammie Palmer case but was, perhaps, because of it.

I sat in the carriage with a set of grey-faced commuters, ill nourished by their ration-book breakfast, facing a day of monotonous grind before returning to their home – if they were lucky enough to have one still – and to another skimpy meal and a night of worry about bombing raids. They all looked as though they were being conveyed to the funeral of a favourite aunt.

The war was only a little over a year old and yet it was very difficult to remember the wonderful normality of peacetime when food was reasonably plentiful, when we could sleep at ease in our own beds at night and simple pleasures were just that and not desperately snatched moments. That Adolf Hitler had a lot to answer for.

Daylight was still fighting for superiority of the sky as I made my way from the tube station to Carlton Street. It was a pleasant, broad thoroughfare which had seen better days. There were a few sorry-looking trees and an air of seediness and decay. It did not take me long to find the house I was looking for. It was a narrow, terraced job with the white paint peeling off the front. There was a light on upstairs but as yet the downstairs was in darkness. I peered in through the window but the curtains were drawn.

Crossing the street, I found myself a little hidy-hole down a narrow passage which afforded me a full view of the house. Once in position I lit up a Craven A and I waited.

Within an hour I had seen what I didn't want to see.

With the leaden weight of disappointment on my shoulders, I headed back to the city and Benny's Café and some sustenance. My mission had been successful in a sense. I had satisfied my suspicions, but I wasn't happy with the outcome. Sometimes I can be too clever for my own good.

'You're a little early for lunch,' said Benny, flicking the crumbs off the table with a tea towel. 'It's good today. Lasagne with some real beef.'

I grinned 'Some?'

Benny gave his shoulders an eloquent shrug. 'Well, you can't have everything.'

'Title of my autobiography.'

'Ah, so you're still carrying the weight of the world around in your shoulders, Mr Johnny One Eye. How about a cup of coffee and a custard tart? That should put you to rights.'

'Custard tart? With *some* real custard I suppose.'

Benny beamed. 'The finest dried egg in London.'

'You've convinced me.' I grinned.

'Be with you in a trice. Oh, say, Johnny, you seen the news today?'

'No. I was up too early for the papers. Don't tell me Hitler's surrendered.'

'We should be so lucky. No, it's in the *Daily Mirror*. That film star you're so fond of ... Gordon Moore.'

'What about him?'

'He's dead.'

A cold shiver advanced its way down my back at speed. 'Dead? How did he die?'

'Says he was murdered.'

So the phantom caller had struck.

'Let me see the paper, will you?'

'Now I'm a library.' He hustled off and came back a few

minutes later with a cup of coffee, a very pale custard tart, and a crumpled copy of the *Daily Mirror*.

True to Gordon Moore's status as second rate B movie actor, the news of his death was reported on page two. There was a picture of him – taken many years ago looking every inch the glamorous hero – with the headline TIGER BLAKE DIES. The story was brief and scant on details:

ARP Warden, George Benson, discovered the dead body of film actor Gordon Moore, star of the Tiger Blake film series, in the gutter on Harwood Street W.1. at around one in the morning. It appeared that the actor had been attacked and had been stabbed several times. It has been established that the motive for the crime was not theft as his wallet and all his personal belongings were still upon his person. The police are treating the death as murder. [*Remarkably perceptive!*] His agent, Bruce Mellor, told our reporter that Mr Moore had been somewhat depressed of late because he had just received the news that he would not be making any more Tiger Blake movies. 'His death is a great loss to British cinema.' said Mr Mellor. Mrs Moore's wife was unavailable for comment. The police are continuing their investigation.

I bit into my custard tart. Not only was its consistency thoroughly disgusting, resembling a kind of yellow mucus, but it was also quite tasteless. I swallowed quickly and took a gulp of coffee. The industrial strength chicory swilled down the offending confectionery.

So poor old Gordon Moore was dead. In meeting his end he had vacated his place in my mental library where I had assembled all the possible culprits – those that I knew about at least. The suspects were thinning out. But why had he been killed? Did he know something, something incriminating? If so, was he aware of it? Or was he killed because he had sullied the flesh of Pammie Palmer? Surely not. He wasn't the only client that she had. And was the person who murdered

Pammie the same one who had stabbed Gordon Moore to death? It was the same *modus operandi*. So many questions and so few answers.

'You didn't finish your tart.' Benny loomed over me benevolently.

'I was just savouring it. Good food should not be rushed.'

'In this you are right. Go ahead ... savour.'

I handed him back the *Daily Mirror*. 'Sad news about Gordon Moore.'

'Sure,' replied Benny, slipping the newspaper under his arm. 'But he had a good life – the film-star life: champagne and girls, the big cars, premieres. What did he know about rationing and trying to run a café on bits of beef, dried eggs and Spam?'

Without waiting for a reply, he headed back to the counter. With his back to me, I took the opportunity of scraping up the remnants of the custard tart, wrapping them in my handkerchief and ramming it in my raincoat pocket out of sight.

It was time to kill two birds with one stone. I took myself off to Bermondsey to see Mr Leo Epstein and I thought I'd invite Eve out for lunch.

Eve didn't seem particularly pleased to see me but I pretended not to notice. Dawn gave a cheery wave and thrust out her chest at me. I waved back with an appreciative leer.

With the curling of my forefinger, I beckoned Eve over so that I could have a quiet conversation with her without being overheard. Reluctantly she came over to me.

'I've got a bit of business with Mr Epstein and then I thought we could grab a sandwich for lunch together,' I said *sotto voce*. 'There must be a decent pub nearby.'

Eve gave me a nervous smile. 'That's very kind of you, Johnny, but I have rather a heavy workload today and—'

I shook my head, smiling as I did so. 'Nonsense. I won't hear any other answer but yes. We have so much to talk about. Things to sort out. I really want to know all about Ray.'

She stared at me in amazement and then instinctively turned

around to check that Dawn hadn't heard, but she was busy filing ... her nails.

'How ...?'

'I am a detective after all,' I said. 'We'll talk about it over lunch.'

She gave me a resigned nod.

'Good.' I gave her my broadest smile. 'Now is the great white chief in?'

'Yes, but you don't have an appointment.'

'Nah, but he'll always see me.'

I gave a sharp rap on the door and entered the sanctum of Leo Epstein.

He was seated at his desk, smoking a large cigar and he looked up in surprise as I entered. His surprise quickly turned into anger.

'What the hell are you doing here?' he cried.

'I've come to do you a favour.'

'I don't want any favours from you.' He was about to leap from his chair and perform the, 'Get out of my office and never sully my doormat again' routine, when I stopped him in his tracks.

'In precise terms, I've come to save your life.'

The cigar dropped from his mouth and fell on to the desk, scorching one of the documents.

twenty-six

'What do you know about Ray?'

Eve leaned close to me so that no one else could hear our conversation. We were in the Coach and Horses, a busy pub off the Bermondsey High Street, huddled around a little table with a couple of drinks and four pieces of bread masquerading as sandwiches. My treat ... in a manner of speaking. The pub was filled with the lunchtime crowd, noisy and self absorbed in the pleasantly fuggy atmosphere. In this strange, timeless haven you'd never think there was a war on. That of course was why it was crowded: it provided a momentary escape from reality. There was no danger of anyone being interested in the conversation between a strange one-eyed man and a pretty young woman.

I winked enigmatically. 'I think I know what's important to know about Ray,' I said, before taking a bite of my dry sandwich. It was an original kind: two pieces of bread with no filling, unless you counted the reddish tissue paper pretending to be corned beef. I certainly didn't count it.

She shook her head in disbelief. 'But how?'

'Well, I smelt a rat – no offence intended – when you got so shirty about me seeing you home the other evening. You had been sweetness and light up to that moment and then suddenly you shut the door on me.'

She sighed. 'Yes, I'm sorry about that. I'd had a little more to drink than I should have, otherwise I would have handled it better.'

'I'm sure you would, Miss Kendal. Anyway, it made me a little suspicious. It niggled me, so I rang up your office yesterday and asked to speak to Dawn. Do you remember a Scottish gentleman by the name of Angus McPherson calling? I put on my best Edinburgh accent.'

'That was you?'

'Aye, my wee lassie, it was me. I spun Dawn, the romantic Dawn, a little tale. I said I wanted to send some flowers to your home and asked her if she would supply me with your address. I said I didn't want you to know. She thought it was a lovely gesture, right out of a soppy novel. She came up with the goods and I swore her to secrecy. She's a good kid.'

Eve smiled in spite of everything. 'I didn't receive any flowers.'

'My apologies. It was a cheap ruse, I'm afraid. Although I suspect it would have been problematic for you if a dozen red roses had turned up on your doorstep with the message, "All my love, Johnny". How would you explain that?'

Eve bit her lip in response.

'You see,' I continued, 'a little research told me that the address I was given is rented by a young couple called Fowler. Eve and Raymond. Now this Raymond is in the army, but he's been reported missing, absent without leave. He has, not to put too fine a point on it, joined the swelling ranks of deserters.'

Eve's eyes misted up and she turned away for a moment while she scrabbled for a handkerchief in her handbag. I waited for her to compose herself.

'Kendal is my maiden name. I've reverted back to it because I no longer consider myself a married woman. Ray and I were seeing each other just before the war started. We hadn't been courting for very long, when suddenly all the men were enlisting and going off to war. Somehow we got caught up with things. All that flag-waving romantic stuff. Oh, it was a terrible mistake. I think we both realized that almost straight away. We planned to split up but then when Ray was conscripted he asked me to wait for him. I couldn't very well say no, could I? There he was about to go off and fight for his king and country and possibly get killed. I couldn't tell him to get lost. We were married, after all.'

I said nothing. I didn't know what my course of action would have been in such a situation, but the thought of being married to a lovely girl like Eve appealed greatly.

'Well, he didn't go off to fight for king and country, did he?' she continued. 'Ray had barely finished his training before he scarpered. He went missing. He claimed he couldn't bear the regimentation of the army. It stifled him, he said, and he thought that all the officers had it in for him.'

Paranoid as well, I thought, but still remained the attentive silent listener. It was a familiar tale. David Llewellyn at the Yard had told me that the numbers of deserters were growing daily. It really was a serious problem with not enough personnel to follow up individual cases. This was well known. In fact it encouraged the practice. A really wily deserter could, in essence, vanish, never to be seen again. With forged ration books and a slight change of appearance, they could slip back into civilian life with great ease. What puzzled me was how they could live with themselves when numbers of their fellow countrymen were dying in the war – men who hadn't given up, but had denied themselves all the comforts of home and the nearness of their loved ones to fight for Britain against the Nazis.

'He was on the run for about three months. At first the officials were round searching the place every week. Looking under the bed and all that. Then when the fuss died down a bit, Ray turned up on the doorstep. He'd grown a moustache and taken to wearing spectacles. He really didn't look like the same man.'

'Tall, blondish hair, prominent nose.'

Eve's eyes widened. 'How do you know?'

'I saw him this morning. He came to the door as you left for work.'

It took a few moments for the import of these words to strike home. 'This morning ... you mean ... you were spying on me? Why you ...!'

She had raised her voice sufficiently to attract the attention of a few of the customers. I placed my forefinger to my lips in a hushing motion. 'Careless talk ...' I said quietly.

Eve was still angry. 'You rat, fancy spying on a person like that. Where were you? Hiding in the dustbin?'

'I was just across the street. And I am a detective, after all. It's my job to find things out. And I had to find out why you were so desperate to prevent me from seeing you home the other evening.'

'I am not a criminal.'

'Well, that's a moot point, Eve. You are harbouring a known deserter on your premises.'

'But he's my husband. You can't expect me to give him up, can you?'

'I don't know. You seem to be able to go on dates with gullible gentlemen despite being married.'

Her eyes watered and she shook her head in dismay. 'In a real sense, the marriage is dead. I don't love him any more. Ray is just a lodger. We are going to get divorced when the war is over.'

'These are mixed messages, Eve. The marriage is over and I can't betray my husband.'

'I know it sounds odd, but surely you can understand. I did *marry* Ray. I thought I loved the man and I just can't ignore that fact. I simply can't betray him by welching to the authorities. I think what he has done is despicable and I've tried to persuade him to go back, but he won't. And I can't do it for him. Surely you can see that?'

'In a way, I suppose,' I said reluctantly, although the thought of anyone supporting a deserter caused me great unease. 'So, that means I have to wait until the end of the war before we can have another date.'

Eve looked away, absently-mindedly turning her glass round and round.

'What are you going to do about Ray?' she asked at length.

Indeed, what was *I* going to do about Ray? Now I knew the situation for certain, if I kept the information to myself I too would be aiding and abetting a deserter.

'He's got to turn himself over to the army.'

'He won't. He can't.'

'Can't!' I sneered. 'Of course he bloody well can. He just needs to get in touch with his guts. He'll spend a few months in a military prison and then be returned to the army. He can request to be transferred to another unit if that's a problem to him. It would be better for him to give himself up rather than be arrested as a deserter.'

'I'll talk to him.'

'You'd better. And be at your persuasive best. Because if he doesn't hand himself over to the authorities, I'll have to do it for him.'

'Would you actually do that?'

I took a drink. Warm, flat beer, ideal for raising the spirits. 'I would. It's my duty. You cannot imagine what I would give to have a chance to fight for my country instead of being this one-eyed reject. I have no sympathy with the Rays of this world.'

'I'll do my best.' She glanced awkwardly at her watch. 'I'd better get back to the office.'

I nodded. 'Yeah, off you go.'

'I'm sorry I messed you around, Johnny. I didn't mean to. I liked you and ... I was lonely.'

'Mmm, lonely with a husband at home.' I shouldn't have said that. It wasn't fair and it was wounding. But I had said it before my brain could warn my mouth. Eve's face told me that she thought it was unfair, too, and that it had hurt her. Without another word, she left, pushing her way through the crowded pub.

twenty-seven

After Eve had departed, I made my way to the bar and ordered another drink. I wanted to think and I always found alcohol an effective lubrication for the rusty cogs in my brain, especially when consumed in a warm, smoky atmosphere where no one knows you. The barmaid, a rosy-faced matron with unnaturally bright blonde hair, smiled at me as she pulled my pint. 'Your lady friend gone?'

I nodded. So she'd noticed. We'd not been as anonymous as I'd thought.

'Not had a tiff, I hope.'

'No, she had to go back to work,' I murmured.

'Lovely looking girl. You two going to get married?'

Had the Gestapo Interrogation Squad infiltrated itself into this part of London, I wondered. Would I suddenly be strapped to a chair and have a bright light shone in my eye? All I wanted was a pint, not to deliver an exposé of my love life.

I forced a shy smile. 'It's early days yet.'

'Go on with yer,' she cried, as though to bring in the other boozers around the bar into the conversation. Luckily, they didn't respond, wrapped up in their own lives and not some passing stranger's. No doubt they had seen all this before. Miss Nosy Parker interrogating an unsuspecting male drinker. However, their indifference did not stop her inquisition. 'I've seen enough courting couples come in here to know when it's a right match or not. You made a very sweet pair and not half.'

'Leave him alone, Rosie,' responded a large chap with a face like a disgruntled bulldog, leaning against the bar, nursing an empty glass. 'Can't you see you're embarrassing the feller.'

'Nonsense,' grinned Nosy Rosie as she passed me the pint. 'You're not bothered, are you, lad?'

'Not really,' I replied, maintaining my shy persona. And then quickly I returned to my seat, wondering why Rosie didn't pay more attention to the state of her sandwiches than to the potential marital status of her customers.

My mind now clouded with this episode, I had to clear it again. So many things had become evident to me in the last twelve hours or so but I was really working on instinct rather than rational and considered thinking. I hoped to goodness I was right in my conclusions. I thought back to my recent interview with Leo Epstein not an hour ago in his luxurious 'I keep the world at bay' office.

I was sure that he had not been to the police to tell them of his relationship with Pammie. Oh no, he would bluff it out. But thanks to Eve, I was aware that his little fling, as he reported it to me, had been a full blown affair, one in which he was the infatuated participant. I had cut through his angry bluster and told him that I knew all about his passionate relationship with Pammie. What a delight it was to see a solicitor lost for words. That must go down in my book as one of the most memorable moments of 1940.

Eventually, the legal mind having recovered its momentum, he addressed me in his courtroom voice. 'Who told you this?'

'It doesn't matter.'

'Oh, yes it does. Was it Eve? If it was, she'll be getting her cards tonight.'

I shook my head and smiled gently as I lied through my teeth. 'Of course it wasn't Eve.'

'Then who?'

'I cannot divulge my source, Mr Epstein,' I said, matching his pompous tone, 'but your reaction to my revelation convinces me that the story is true.'

'Of course it's true. I loved Pammie. I'd never met anyone like her before. She was beautiful, alluring, sexy and yet somehow spiritual.'

He made her sound like a lady's perfume.

'And you paid her for sex.'

Momentarily Epstein shifted awkwardly in his chair and his face flushed with anger but he quickly regained his composure. 'It wasn't like that. Wasn't like that at all. I don't suppose I can expect you to understand. Yes, I bought her presents, paid for things, took her to nice places. But I did it willingly. I was happy to do so because it made her happy and that made me happy. There was no formal financial arrangement. No contract – if that's what you were thinking. I just gave her some money from time to time.'

'You paid for sex,' I affirmed.

'That's all it reduces down to in your gutter of a mind doesn't it, Hawke? Some kind of prostitution. Well, it wasn't. If it was only about sex, I could have had many other girls for less expenditure. Can't you get it through your thick skull, I cared about her? I would have married her if she'd have had me.'

'So why did you kill her?'

His reaction was not the one I expected. He didn't explode. His jaw didn't drop like it does with characters in novels who are unexpectedly accused of a heinous crime. He didn't cry. He didn't try to thump the living daylights out of me. And he didn't confess. Instead he shook his head wearily and rather sadly. 'I would not have harmed a hair of Pammie's head. I could no more kill her than I could my own mother.'

'Well, they say matricide is on the increase.'

Epstein sneered at me. 'Call yourself a detective. You wouldn't know a murder suspect if he jumped up and confessed.'

I lit a cigarette. 'Actually, I do know that you didn't kill Pammie but I reckon it's always worth asking the question. It's possible I could be wrong.'

'If you don't think I killed Pammie, why are you harassing me with your questions and your nasty innuendos? Why aren't you out there trying to find the bastard who did commit the crime?'

'I already know and that's why I am here.' I blew the smoke into the air and watched it as it spiralled towards the ceiling before disappearing.

'Explain yourself.'

'Are you ready for this? I believe that the person who killed Pammie, also killed Gordon Moore, the actor.'

'You mean the chap who plays Tiger Blake?

'That's the feller. He was murdered last night. Stabbed to death. Like Pammie.'

'You've lost me already. What's Gordon Moore to do with all this?'

'He was another of her lovers. And like yourself he fell in love with her.'

Epstein shook his head in bewilderment. 'I still don't understand....'

'I believe our murderer wanted to possess Pammie. To own her. She was too good for any other man to touch. When he couldn't prevent her from indulging in her ... what shall we call them? ... amorous activities, he killed her and then set about getting rid of her lovers as a punishment for sullying her flesh. He couldn't touch Sam Fraser because he was arrested immediately and anyway, as things stand, he's likely to end up on the gallows. So he turned his attention to the others. Gordon Moore was more accessible than Fraser and so, my friend, are you.'

'Me?'

'I believe that you are next on the list.'

'Isn't this a bit melodramatic?'

'Of course it is – but murder is melodramatic. The thing that invades a person's psyche and drives them to take someone's life is weird and fantastic. The belief that by shedding blood you are righting a wrong or easing a pain is beyond moral consciousness. There is insanity there – and insanity above all things is melodramatic.'

Epstein looked a little chastened after my outburst which in its own way, I must admit, was somewhat melodramatic also. 'Who is this person?'

'Not yet. I'm keeping that piece of information to myself.'

'But the police should know.'

'Indeed, they should, but at present they have shut their ears and eyes to any other explanations regarding Pammie Palmer's death because they believe that they have the man responsible. And you will not shift that rock of belligerence – I refer to Chief Inspector Knight – in this conviction. It would ruin his record if it turned out to be someone else, someone other than his chosen victim.'

'So you're going it alone.' Epstein couldn't keep the sneer from his voice, not that I supposed he wanted to.

I nodded.

'It just doesn't make sense. Are you telling me that my life is in danger?'

'I believe so.'

'But why me? How does the killer know about me?'

'Of that I'm not sure. There probably was a diary which he found at Pammie's flat.'

'There must be others on the list then. She had quite a few clients I believe.'

'But none like you and Gordon Moore. You didn't just have sex with Pammie, you formed a relationship with her. It wasn't casual or anonymous sex, there were feelings involved on both sides.'

'Whoever this person is must have been very close to Pammie. Someone who knew her secrets.'

'Yes.'

'How did you find out about Moore?'

'Sam Fraser gave me some names of Pammie's clients. He was top of the list. I met Gordon Moore yesterday. He was a sad case: a film actor on the skids with a frigid wife. He found some warmth and affection with her. He visited her the night she was killed.'

'What?'

'He was the one who found her body.'

'My God!'

'And now he's dead. Stabbed to death. All because he loved Pammie.'

Epstein's features paled and with an unsteady hand he reached for the decanter of brandy on the table behind him. He poured himself a large measure and gulped it down. 'So according to you some maniac is on the loose and I'm next on his list? Is that what you're saying?'

'You sum the situation most succinctly.'

'Then I must have police protection.'

I threw Epstein a grim smile. 'They'll just laugh at you.'

'What do you suggest then? I simply wait like some tethered goat until this madman tries to kill me?'

'I suppose I am suggesting that.' I held up my hand to silence Epstein's protests. 'Now wait a minute and hear me out,' I snapped. 'You describe our murderer as mad and ... yes that is probably true. But he is a cunning one. Now his blood is up and he's aware that he cannot get away without being caught for much longer, he'll feel the need to strike soon very soon.'

'That's a great comfort.'

'Cuts down on the waiting time.'

'I get the impression that you are enjoying this, Hawke.'

'Far from it, but I am trying to be realistic. Now, what are your plans after closing up the office tonight?'

Epstein gave me a nervous glance. 'Tonight! As soon as that! Tonight. You really think....'

'Yes, I do.'

'Christ almighty!' He brushed his hand across his high forehead which was beginning to moisten with perspiration. 'What a nightmare.'

'So ... what had you intended to do?' I prompted.

Epstein shook his head distractedly. 'I ... I hadn't given it much thought. I don't know. Probably I was going to work late a little and then grab a bite to eat. Maybe a trip to the cinema and then go home.'

'No lady friend to meet?' I raised a disappointed eyebrow.

'Not at the moment.'

'Pity. I don't think our man would strike if you were accompanied. I reckon the best thing is for you to do as you say – a meal and the flicks. Act as normal and I shall be in the shadows watching you.'

'You mean I act as bait? You must be off your head. I'm going to call the police.' His hand shot out and snatched up the receiver. The buzzing noise seemed unnaturally loud and filled the silent room. I made no move to stop him but as his finger hooked into the dial, I leaned forward with a steady stare.

'What exactly are you going to say? How are you going to explain things?' I said, softly.

He seemed on the verge of responding to my questions but then gave up the effort. Slowly, he replaced the receiver and the buzzing noise ceased.

Leo Epstein sat back in his chair, his shoulders bowed and his face a grim mask of despair. 'It would seem that I have no choice,' he said in a monotone.

'That's how I see things,' I said in cheery agreement.

As I came to the closing moments of the re-run of this interview in my mind, old Nosy Rosie, the barmaid with the inquisitive demeanour, came to my table to empty the ashtray and wipe a damp cloth over the top. 'By Jove, love,' she smiled, leaning close to me so that I could smell her cheap perfume and see further into the chasm of her ample cleavage, 'for a feller who's in love, you've got a face like a wet weekend.'

'They run in my family.'

'Well, if you ever need cheering up, just let Rosie know.'

'Certainly will,' I said, retreating once again into my false shyness.

Without another word she gave me a wink and swept on to the next table. When she had her back to me, I skipped out of the pub in search of anonymity again – and some peace in which to think.

It had begun to rain, that rain which falls like a fine mesh curtain and soaks you through to the skin. Pulling up my collar and tugging my hat forward, I walked, trying hard to calm the panic of uncertainty which was growing inside me. What if I was wrong in my conclusions? What if I had figured out the situation all wrong? When it came down to it, it was only my personal interpretation of events and maybe I'd misread the signs. Maybe.

I was no Sherlock Holmes. I had not made any major brain-leap deductions. There could really only be one possible culprit for the murders – couldn't there? It was just that Chief Inspector Knight and his gang had closed their minds to any other interpretations of the facts. And it was left up to me to pin the tail on this murdering donkey. And the only way to do that was to catch the bugger on the job. He must know his days were numbered and so he had to strike soon if he was to kill Epstein, the third man who had cared for and yet used *his* daughter.

twenty-eight

Sister Susan McAndrew waited in the corridor. She was filled with apprehension, although in her heart of hearts she knew the outcome. Nervously she fingered the slip of paper that John Hawke had given her the day before. He'd seemed a nice chap and genuinely concerned about the boy.

In the dim corridor she could hear the muffled noises of the hospital: the creak of the trolleys, the slamming of doors, hushed conversations, the hum of some machine or other and the occasional cry of pain. It was the backdrop to her life; she couldn't imagine being without it.

Eventually Dr Walker and a grey-faced man in the smart double-breasted suit emerged from the private ward. Their faces were expressionless, but she knew what decision had been made.

Sister McAndrew stepped forward and smiled, using this as a prompt for the two men to pass on the information, to confirm her worst fears about Peter.

The grey-faced man who had been introduced to her briefly as Mr Stanley ignored her as though she didn't register with him at all, but Dr Walker smiled at his colleague. He knew that she cared desperately about the boy and had formed a strong attachment to him. This, if anything, was the only weakness that Sister McAndrew had in her nursing duties. She cared too much. She lacked the ability to treat patients with kindness and attention while maintaining a distance. She became too much involved. Caring too much really was a weakness. It could only bring about greater stress and reduced efficiency. However, he mused, he supposed that it was better this way than the rather

harsh and brusque nature of some of the older nurses who had
been coaxed out of retirement to help during this time of war.
They were martinets of the old school and if brow-beating a
patient into health was a scientific technique, they were
masters, or rather mistresses of it.

Walker returned McAndrew's smile. 'Well, Sister,' he said
kindly, 'the boy has made a splendid recovery thanks, no doubt,
to your ministrations. And so he's ready to move on. Mr
Stanley believes he can find a place for him at Moorfield House
– that's a boys' home out Windsor way. Isn't that right, Mr
Stanley?'

The grey-faced man deigned to acknowledge this with a curt
nod. 'I see no point in delaying matters,' he said, his voice
strangely hollow and without character or inflection.
'Obviously, the boy is hiding the truth about his background,
but short of beating it out of him there's no way we can
discover more about his origins. If he says his parents are dead
then we just have to accept that. I'm not going to sanction more
time and effort in a futile attempt to investigate further. We
have too many orphans to deal with as it is, without causing
ourselves extra trouble for a snivelling little liar.'

Sister McAndrew flinched at Stanley's description of Peter.
The phrase seemed to sum up how far this man had hardened
his heart to the tasks of dealing with orphans. She would have
liked to have put the man right, telling him that Peter was a
lovely boy but was damaged, disturbed by something in his past
which haunted him and which he tried to blot out from his
memory. He wasn't 'a snivelling little liar' but a brave and
frightened casualty of the terrible times they were living
through. He needed kindness, attention and, above all, time to
come to terms with a life without a mother or a father. He was
not going to get that of course. He was to be bundled up and
taken to Moorfield, an institution for parentless children where
the facilities of kindness, comforts and attention were in sparse
supply. Whatever frying pan poor Peter had fallen out of, he
was about to land in the fire.

'I see. When is this to take place?'

Stanley sniffed. 'As soon as possible. I will need to speak to the matron at Moorfield this evening to verify that we have a bed for the boy. Once that is settled, I can arrange for his transfer some time tomorrow. I'm sure, Doctor, that you'll be pleased for this to happen as soon as possible. No doubt you'll have sore need of the bed....'

'We certainly do,' nodded Dr Walker.

'Right, then, it's settled. I'll call first thing in the morning with details.' Without a glance at Sister McAndrew, he turned and strode off down the corridor, his brightly polished shoes squeaking, almost as in protest.

Dr Walker sighed as he looked at the miserable features of Sister McAndrew. He touched her gently on the shoulder. 'None of this, please,' he said briskly. 'We've done our bit. There are more casualties on the conveyor belt needing our attention.'

'I know,' she said softly. 'I'll just pop in to see if Peter wants anything, then I'll get back to the ward.'

Peter was reading a comic when Sister McAndrew came into the room. He looked up eagerly with expectation, his pale shiny features spotlighted by the bedside lamp. He tried not to show his disappointment when he saw that she was his visitor.

'I ... I thought you might be Johnny. He said he'd come today. He was going to bring me a Tiger Blake comic.'

Sister McAndrew smiled in spite of herself. 'Well, today's not over with yet, I suppose. I'm sure he's not forgotten. If he doesn't get here today, no doubt he'll be round to see you in the morning.' She hoped so, or he'd miss the boy altogether before he was carted off to Moorfield House. She had rung John Hawke twice that afternoon when she knew that Mr Stanley was coming and all that his visit implied, but there was no reply.

'You like Mr Hawke ... Johnny ... don't you?' she said, plumping up the boy's pillows.

'He's ... all right,' answered Peter, with the shy reserve of the young. And then added, more naturally, 'He makes me laugh.'

Sister McAndrew gave a weary smile. 'Ah, that's a rare gift these days.'

There was something about the nurse's behaviour that suddenly worried Peter. Her tone, her stance were different somehow. Something had made her unhappy and she was trying to hide it.

'Are they sending me away?' he asked, with a sudden cold realization.

Peter's face was pale and frightened. There was desperate hope and fear evident in his expression as he sat up in bed and grasped Sister McAndrew's hand.

'Ssh, now,' she said gently. 'There's no need to fret. Everything's going to be all right.'

Peter gasped and shook his head. 'I don't want to go away. I'm happy here.'

Sister McAndrew could not help but smile. 'But you don't want to live the rest of your life in a hospital, do you?'

'Yes,' he cried, tears welling up in his eyes.

'Now that's silly. You're better now. They'll find a nice place for you to stay where you can be looked after with children of your own age.'

'A prison?'

Sister McAndrew ran her cool hand over the boy's forehead. 'No, of course not. Prison is a place for naughty people. You haven't done anything wrong, have you?'

Peter shook his head, the terrible gravity of his situation slowly sinking in. He would be taken to a children's home and his life would be over. He knew it. He had read of such places in his comics and they were prisons. He would be beaten and fed on bread and water. He bit his lip; he bit it hard to prevent further tears trickling down his cheek.

'Are you sure Johnny ... hasn't been here today?' he said eventually, when he felt he had his emotions under control.

'Not yet, but I'm sure he wouldn't deliberately let you down.'

This platitude cut no ice with Peter. He had been roughly handled most of his life. He had heard promises and excuses galore from his mother. He could sense a lie or a desperate cover up when he heard one. So, even Johnny, whom he was really beginning to like, had turned out just like the rest. This revelation hardened his heart and with a gesture of bravado, he wiped his tears away.

'I'm tired,' he said, softly. He wanted the nurse to go, to leave him to think things over. She was a nice lady but he knew that she could do nothing to help him.

Once again she ran her cool fingers across his brow. 'Of course,' she said in a cooing fashion. 'You get a good night's sleep. Everything will seem a lot better in the morning.'

He didn't reply, but just snuggled further down under the covers. Already his eyelids were fluttering. Sister McAndrew leaned forward and planted a gentle kiss on his forehead. Her heart ached for the little boy and she cursed herself for being too sensitive.

As he she reached the door, she turned and saw that already Peter was fast asleep. For some reason a fragment of poetry floated into her mind – some lines of Shakespeare she had learned at school: *sleep that knits up the ravelled sleeve of care.* And so it does, she thought, but with morn's early light the whole thing is unravelled again.

With a heavy heart, she closed the door.

Within seconds, Peter's bright eyes were wide open. Silently, he slipped from the bed and opened the cabinet beside it, the one which contained his clothes.

twenty-nine

I had just positioned myself in the doorway almost adjacent to Epstein's offices when I remembered.

Peter!

I was meant to visit Peter in the hospital and take him some comics. I muttered an oath under my breath. How could I have forgotten? I had been so wrapped up in my own concerns about Eve and the bloody Pammie Palmer case that I had let the matter of Peter slip my mind completely. I was disgusted with myself. I had betrayed his trust. I had let the lad down – like others in his past. Those who had driven him to roam the streets, sleeping in doorways and denying memories of any previous existence. I was no better than them.

I imagined Peter, sitting up in bed, his eyes trained on the door expecting a visit from his new friend clutching a whole batch of comics, including some Tiger Blake ones. Every time the door opened, his expectations would rise and then be dashed. And it was my fault. My failure. And I, above all, the miserable orphan with the one eye, should have known better – should have cared more.

I would have to get to the hospital as soon as I could tomorrow and hope that it wasn't too late to repair the damaged emotional bridges. At the thought of my failings in this matter, I felt a heavy weight settle upon my senses. If any good was to come out of this whole wretched affair it would be the emotional rehabilitation of Peter and I had already thrown a spanner into the works. I cursed myself again.

It was around five o'clock and still raining. I huddled into my damp raincoat and lit a cigarette. Across the road I observed the lights go on in the Epstein offices. I could see thin streaks of illumination visible at the edge of the blackout curtains. If the ARP warden had seen those, there'd be trouble.

It had been agreed with Epstein that after Eve and Dawn had left the premises for the evening, he would stay on for another fifteen minutes before locking up. It was then my job to tail him while he went for a meal and took a trip to the cinema before going home. All this in the expectation that the murderer would at some point have a go at him. It was my job to see that he didn't succeed.

I was well aware that this wasn't a foolproof plan but it should – I hoped – bring about a swift conclusion to the case. It should. But then again, this particular mongrel could be baying against the incorrect arboreal growth.

Just after 5.30, Eve and Dawn appeared on the street. They chatted for a while sheltering from the rain under a shop awning and then they went their separate ways. Eve, her face drawn and miserable, walked past me on the other side of the street, oblivious of my presence in the doorway. Her shoulders were hunched against the rain and her whole demeanour was one of misery as though she was withdrawing into herself. No doubt she wasn't relishing the thought of telling her husband what had happened today and how he had little choice but to give himself up and return to his regiment.

With a sharp click, clack of her heels on the wet pavement, she disappeared down the street and out of sight. I wanted to go after her, kiss her and give her all the support that I could. But it wasn't possible. It wouldn't be right. And I had a job to do.

As the clock ticked on, both the traffic and pedestrians diminished. By 6.00, all the shops had closed down and the street was almost deserted. There was no sign of Leo Epstein. The thin shafts of light at the windows of his office told me that he was still there. Or to be precise, that someone was there. Then another thought struck me: all it meant was that the lights were on.

I began to grow uneasy.

By 6.30, I knew it was time for some action. Checking carefully that there were no suspicious loiterers abroad, I left my hiding place and crossed the road. The office door of Leo Epstein was locked of course, but with my trusty strand of wire and a steady hand, I soon had it open. I let myself in and with a pocket torch in one hand and my old revolver in the other I made my way up the darkened stairway. At the top there was another locked door. I rapped on the glass panel and called out.

'Hello,' I cried.

There was no reply.

A combination of irritation and concern prompted me to smash the glass panel in the door with the butt of my revolver. This allowed me to see into the empty illuminated office beyond, but the recalcitrant door remained locked.

I called out again. 'Epstein?' My cry was swallowed up by the shelves of dusty legal papers.

And there was still no reply.

I was too concerned at this unexpected turn of events and too impatient to use my wire to tackle the lock so I used another less sophisticated technique to open the door: my right shoulder and brute force. With a sudden crack, the door swung wide. I stood for a moment on the threshold and waited to see if the noise had roused anyone. It didn't; the office was as silent as the grave.

I crossed to Epstein's office and opened the door. The lights were on but the room was empty. There was a cigar butt in the ashtray on his desk. I examined it. It was still warm. Clearly my friend Leo had not been gone for too long. But gone he was. But where to? And how? I had been waiting outside the premises for over an hour and a half and I'd swear that he had not left.

I tipped my hat back with the barrel of my pistol as I'd seen John Wayne do in countless westerns and pondered my problem. Then my own words came back to me ... 'he had not left.' Well, he had not left *by the door that I was watching*. But he had obviously departed the building ... so logically, there must be another means of exit. Elementary, my dear Watson. I gazed around the room. At the rear, in the shadows was a curtained recess.

I pulled the curtain back and revealed a door. It was built of stout metal, not a candidate for my shoulder this time. The lock was ancient and rusty and it took me a good ten minutes of waggling and cajoling with my wire before I heard the satisfying rasp and click as the aged mechanism conspired with the wire to withdraw the bolt.

The door opened out on to a fire escape at the back of the building which led down to a small yard. So that's how my solicitor friend had made his getaway. But why on earth did he feel the need to? What prompted him to ditch our plan – well, my plan, I suppose – and hightail it to heavens knew where? Was he just frightened or did he have a different agenda?

Gingerly, I descended the decrepit metal stairway, training my torch on the steps to aid me. Eventually I reached terra firma and was no wiser. The yard was empty. A gate led to a back alley which was silent and deserted.

With my tail between my legs I returned to Epstein's office. Maybe I could find some indication as to why Leo had flown the nest and where exactly he had flown to. Once inside, after closing the fire escape door, I ran my eye around the room. The first thing it lit upon was the brandy decanter on top of the filing cabinet. Well, I reckoned, the wily old bastard owed me a drink, so I poured myself a large one. The brandy burned my throat and filled my body with a warm glow. I then set about looking around for clues, for some suggestion as to where Epstein could have had gone. I scrutinized his desk. Were there any little scraps of paper bearing an address or a telephone number? There were not. Neither were there any indentations on the blotter that I could shade in with a HB pencil to reveal some telling detail. There was nothing. But then this wasn't a film – it was real life.

And then something very surprising happened. Just as I was eyeing up the brandy decanter, considering whether to treat myself to another slug – the telephone rang.

The shrill noise shattered the strange silence of Epstein's inner sanctum.

I stared hypnotized at the black bakelite machine as it vibrated on the desk. It was as though the thing were alive.

I broke my own trance and grabbed the receiver.

'Hello,' I said.

'Ah, Mr Epstein, still working late?' The voice was tinny and strange. Obviously, it was deliberately disguised.

'Yes. Who is this?' I responded, keeping my own voice a little faint and attempting as much as possible to sound like the absent solicitor.

'A friend, you might say.'

'Does this friend have a name?'

'You will find out soon enough.'

'What do you want?' I tried to sound angry and on the verge of putting the phone down.

'It's about your affair with Pammie Palmer....'

I remained silent, but the skin at the back of my neck began to tingle.

'I think you need my help,' the voice came again.

'Oh, yes. Why?'

The voice chuckled. 'To save you from the gallows. I have some pretty incriminating evidence that links you with the dead girl.'

'I didn't kill her.'

'Maybe not, but the police might think differently. In fact, I'm certain they will.'

'What is this evidence?'

'I think we should meet up to discuss it.'

'What is there to discuss?'

'Money, Mr Epstein. Money.'

'So this is blackmail.'

'Of course.'

'But I don't have any money on me now.'

'Oh, I'm sure you have ways and means of securing a thousand pounds.'

I nearly dropped the receiver at the mention of this amount. How would little old Leo have so much money at his beck and call.

'That's ridiculous,' I said, playing for time.

'Now don't try to fool me, Mr Epstein. I know for certain you have your own private store of cash hidden away for a rainy day. Well, it looks like it's pouring. Let me put it this way: it's either the money or I go to the police.'

I had to play along with the game. 'Very well. I'll get the money but first I need to know what incriminating evidence you have against me.'

'You must wait. But trust me, it is quite damning.'

'Where shall I see you and when?'

'At Pammie's flat at midnight. Be there with the money – or it really will be the worse for you.'

The line went dead.

thirty

The blow sent Eve Kendal crashing to the floor. The blood from her cut lip was already dripping from her chin as she shuffled backwards on her haunches, staring up at her attacker. She was shocked but she was not frightened. A faint sense of indignant righteousness began to rise within her.

'You bitch,' he cried, anger flushing his pale, haunted features. 'You're my wife and you've behaved like a whore!'

Eve had been on the verge of tears but this reference to 'wife' further fuelled her resistance. 'The marriage is over, you know that,' she said with quiet defiance.

'You're my wife. You married me for better or worse.' He spat the words out while he stood over her, clenching and unclenching his fists.

'I'm your wife on paper only – not for real, Ray. There's no love. I told you that long ago. That's why we sleep in separate beds. That's why we have separate lives. You can hit me all you want, but it will not change how I feel about you.'

'You're a married woman and you've been seeing other men.'

'For company. What kind of life have you left me? I'm lonely. I need company.'

'There's me.'

'Yes, there's you skulking behind the curtains watching and waiting. Expecting a knock at the door at any moment. Expecting they've come for you. Come to take you back. That's what you're reduced to. Morose, uncommunicative you.' She wiped the blood off her chin. 'Well, I suppose you can communicate in one way.'

Ray ran his fingers through his hair. 'I never meant to hit you. I didn't want to hurt you.'

'No,' she said, pulling herself to her feet, 'but you did.'

'I'm sorry ...' He made a move to embrace her, but she shrank back.

'Get away,' she said. 'Don't touch me.'

'Please,' he cried, tears moistening his eyes.

'You're a coward, Ray. If things don't go your way, you run away ... or you lash out. It's time you faced up to things. Our marriage was a mistake. Our love affair was just summer lightning. We're strangers really. I've accepted that and I want to move on ... get on with the rest of my life. And you should do, too. You can't go on hiding from the truth ... or your responsibilities ... for ever.'

As she talked in a steady, confident tone, she found her own strength returning and the fear of Ray dissipating. She rose to her feet to face him.

'Go back to the army. You've broad shoulders – let them bear your responsibility. I don't – I don't want to end up hating you.'

Tears fell down Ray's face and he seemed to shrink visibly before her. He shook his head gently. 'You don't seem to realize: I've never, never stopped loving you.'

A cynical smile touched Eve's features. 'Your own selfish version of love.'

'It's the only kind I know.' Suddenly he sneered at her and the old aggression revived in his moist eyes. She thought for a moment he was going to hit her again but instead, he turned on his heel and strode out of the room, slamming the door behind him.

For a moment she stared at the door as though in a trance and then she slumped into an armchair, all her courage and resilience spent. Burying her head in her arm she sobbed quietly.

In a while, she dried her eyes while her mind raced through the limited options she had now.

Suddenly the door burst open and Ray came back in the room carrying with him an empty suitcase. His expression and his stance told Eve that he had recovered his bluster. His frustration had turned into anger once more.

He flung the suitcase at Eve.
'Get packed,' he snarled. 'We're leaving.'

thirty-one

As I left Epstein's office, I could already hear the drone of aircraft in the dark skies above me. The Luftwaffe. Another evening raid. Earlier than usual. No doubt they were heading for the docks for rich pickings, but inevitably the bastards dropped bombs anywhere that took their fancy. There was no such thing as a wasted bomb. Low morale was just as effective to our enemy as low supplies and there was nothing guaranteed to lower morale more than having your house flattened by a Nazi bomb.

That dreaded noise meant more deaths, more damage to the city and more heartache for its inhabitants. Within the hour the public shelters would be crammed with Londoners preparing for another night of unrest, wondering whether they would have a home to go to once the all clear was sounded.

The streets would soon be empty and buses and taxis would be non existent. It looked like I'd have to make my way to Pammie's flat on foot. I checked my watch. It was nearing eight o'clock. That gave me four hours to cross London to make my rendezvous with the mystery caller and, hopefully, come face to face with the killer. My geography of London was fairly sound and I knew that it would take me all my time to make it from Bermondsey to Regent's Park by midnight. I set off with a will, striding out along the empty street.

It had stopped raining and the air was still carrying with it the wail of sirens. The wavering silver shafts of the searchlights scanned the darkness for the enemy aircraft. When they were spotted, like bats flying across the beam of a torch, there came the *boom boom* of the ack ack guns. In the distance I could see the skyline aglow with an orange hue. There had been a hit – a palpable hit.

As I tramped along, I felt a kind of futility in my own mission. Here I was after the murderer of a few tainted individuals, while overhead, way out of reach, were killers of hundreds, maybe thousands of innocent people. By the end of the night, there would be many corpses and casualties littering the rubble of bombed buildings – lives blighted by the German Air Force – by the war. It made the murder of a high-class prostitute and her lovers seem so insignificant.

For a moment I thought back to those halcyon days before the war, when I was a raw constable, a raw constable with two eyes and a naïve faith in the shining future. It was a time of endless summers, an ease of living, certainty of values and relaxed happy-go-lucky communities. It all seemed like a dream now – like a fantasy movie. A sort of British *Lost Horizon*. Once again we had been dragged beyond the confines of our own particular Shangri La, as we had been before in 1914, to face the bleakness and hardship of conflict.

As I walked on, a solitary figure in the darkness, heading towards that false dawn of flames and destruction on the rim of the horizon, it was as though I were the last Londoner left alive. It was only the moan of sirens and the angry chatter of the ack ack guns that told me otherwise.

Suddenly the air was filled with a fierce screeching sound, followed by the growling roar of an explosion. The ground shook beneath my feet and buildings around me seemed to shimmer and melt as in a mirage. Thunder assailed my ears and I threw myself on to the pavement and covered my head as a shower of masonry cascaded down upon me. The Hun had made a direct hit on a large building at the corner of the street some hundred yards ahead of me. An office block, I thought. Flames now shot up from its innards spiralling skywards through the shattered roof. Some of the walls caved in, throwing up clouds of powdery dust to mingle with the conflagration. I lay still for a while hoping it was all over. Hoping that another brute of a bomb didn't land on me. I waited and nothing happened. There was just the roar of the flames and the crack of timbers resonating in my ears. Eventually, I pulled myself to my feet. I was still in one piece. With a silent prayer I shook off the light debris that clung to my coat and gazed around me. The building that had been hit was now standing like a single ragged black tooth against the flames that were intent on consuming it. Nobody would be working in that office again. Drawing nearer through the dust and flames, I could see a dark tableau of filing cabinets, desks and other office equipment mangled and scorched amid mounds of grey and red rubble and charred documents. Flakes of soot floated in the air like funereal snow.

In the distance I could hear the clanging bell of an ancient fire engine. What help that was possible was on its way. The emergency services would be stretched to their limits for yet another night. And when they arrived, what could one do but put the flames out to stop them spreading, and then weep.

One thing was certain, I could be of no help. And the last thing the brigade men needed at this time was a watcher in the shadows. As this phrase came into my mind – 'watcher in the shadows' – it reverberated in my brain like an electric shock. Some bright light fizzed and arched across from one pole to another like the equipment in *The Bride of Frankenstein* or the Flash Gordon serials and an enlightening connection was made. Watcher in the shadows. That phrase unlocked something. Veils were lifted.

Of course.

How would my homicidal friend who called me at Epstein's office know that anyone would be there at the late hour when he rang? He knew, I answered myself with some excitement, because he had been watching ... in the shadows. Keeping an eye on the building. Checking on the movements of their victim. And if that were the case – and I was convinced that it was – then the caller would know it was me and not Epstein who had answered the phone. He would have seen me break in and deduce that dear old Leo had flown the coop. All that stuff about incriminating evidence and the rendezvous at Pammie's flat was a load of guff concocted for my benefit. My homicidal friend was misdirecting me. Getting me out of the way, sending me on a wild goose chase while he could deal with Leo Epstein without my interference.

I had been as dim as a blackout curtain!

I was convinced there would be only one place where Epstein would be: his flat. Where he had wanted to go in the first place. Unfortunately the murderer would have guessed that too. Here was a Tiger Blake situation all right. Could I reach the endangered solicitor in time? I glanced at my watch. I had lost about half an hour. Pulling out my wallet, I extracted Epstein's private card which I'd picked up in his office. His address was Flat 14, Cedar Court, Holborn. I really would have to get my skates on.

It was nearing ten o'clock when the skies appeared to be clear again. The Germans had done their dirty on us and returned to base for a late supper. There would be a lot of clanking steins that night I had no doubt.

It was about this time that my luck turned. There ahead of me, lying on the pavement I saw a bicycle. I supposed that it had been abandoned by its owner when the bombing started. Technically, I knew it was stealing and I could easily find myself in prison for looting, but in 'borrowing' the bike, I could ensure that I reached my destination on time. I took no time to hesitate or discuss the moral dilemma with myself; I snatched up the bike and jumped board. Moments later I was pedalling away, in a rather unsteady fashion.

I had not ridden a bike for about ten years but after five minutes of acclimatization, man and machine were one. I pedalled on, instinct and good luck guiding me. Soon I was in Southwark catching glimpses of the river, and then riding across a deserted Blackfriars Bridge towards the city, which appeared like a silhouetted frieze before me, illuminated at irregular intervals with flames, marking the direct hits of the Luftwaffe.

A clock was chiming eleven as I headed up Farringdon Street. I was now making good time. I'd be at Cedar Court within half an hour.

thirty-two

Peter treated it like a game. He was Tiger Blake trapped in a Nazi prison for British spies. It was his job to escape without being spotted. Sneak out right under the noses of those devilish Germans. If he didn't he would be shot at dawn. His tummy churned with pleasurable excitement at the thought of his mission. He was now fully dressed in his own clothes; he had stuffed the faded pyjamas he'd been wearing under the covers of the hospital bed with a couple of pillows so that anyone casually putting their head round the door would think he was still there and fast asleep. He'd seen Tiger do that in *Tiger Blake and the Devil's Gate.*

Holding his breath, he opened the door of his room a fraction, just enough for him to see if the coast was clear. It was. With a deep breath, he slipped out of the room and headed down the corridor. He had no idea which was the best direction to take, the one that would lead him to the exit, but he reckoned his first priority was to get away as far as possible from his room and the people in the vicinity who would know who he was. He reasoned that no one would know him in other parts of the building – after all he wasn't dressed like a patient any more – and if he couldn't see a sign to tell him how to reach the way out, he could, if necessary, ask. If he were really Tiger Blake and this was a German prison, he would have to adopt a German accent and say *Heil Hitler* a lot, but as he sped down the apparently endless corridor, the reality of his situation was overtaking his fantasy. This really was about him, Peter, escaping from a life in an orphanage.

At last he came upon a staircase. A sign indicated ward

numbers with various arrows. That's all. He reckoned it would be best to go down rather than up. As he reached the floor below, he encountered two young nurses coming up. They were engaged in a deep, hushed conversation and did not give the young boy a second glance. Peter grinned. See, he was as clever as Tiger Blake. He went down a further floor and then spotted a sign – a painted hand on the wall pointing and below it the word 'Outpatients'. Peter was unsure what this meant, but was cheered by the 'out' bit. He headed in the direction indicated by the painted pointing hand. Now the corridors were getting cluttered, with wheelchairs, trolleys and occasionally large tanks like those that deep sea divers wore when they were seeking lost treasure at the bottom of the ocean.

As he turned a corner, he collided with a tall man wearing a brown canvas coat, a hospital porter.

'Hey up, sonny. Watch where you're going,' he said, placing his hands on Peter's shoulders and holding him firmly. 'Now then, where are you off to in such a hurry?'

He had a kindly face with swirly white hair and rosy cheeks, but his eyes stared at Peter suspiciously. 'I ... I ... er, was trying to catch my dad up. I got lost. He's waiting for me by the out bit.'

'The out bit? You mean the exit.'

'Yes, that's it. He's waiting there. I ... I sort of wandered off and got a bit lost.'

'A bit lost.' The man's eyes narrowed. 'You certainly did, sonny.'

'Can you tell me how to get to the out ... the exit?'

'Well, this place is a bit of a maze. I think it would be better if I took you there myself. Make sure you meet up with your dad. No doubt he's getting worried about you now.'

Peter nodded. His instinct was to run, but something held him back from this form of action, kept him calm and logical. To run off now would only alarm this chap and then his chances of escaping would be reduced further. He reasoned that he should let him take him to the exit and then he would have to think again. That would be the time to run for it, rather than now. That's what Tiger Blake would have done.

Peter nodded again. 'Thank you, mister,' he said in his most angelic voice.

The porter's eyes softened and he smiled. 'Come on then,' he said kindly, guiding Peter with one hand on his shoulder. They travelled down a whole series of anonymous corridors, some were deserted, some bustling with life, with white-coated doctors and nurses hurrying by. At last, pushing through a pair of swing doors, they came into a large circular foyer which was busy with lots of people, many of whom were neither doctors nor nurses. This must be the exit place, thought Peter, because there were windows. They were shrouded with blackout curtains but they must look out on the real world beyond this infernal Nazi prison. The real world – and it was so close to him now.

'Well, here we are, sonny,' said the porter. 'Now where's your dad?'

'He said he'd be by the door.'

'Ah, over there then.' The porter pointed and at last, Peter spied his escape. As luck would have it, there was a tall man with grizzled features standing by the door checking his watch.

Now he had to chance it. To be brave and full of cleverness like good old Tiger. He wasn't just escaping from the building but from a life of misery in an orphanage where he would be beaten and starved. He slipped from the porter's gentle grip and ran towards the grizzled man with a cry of, 'Dad!'

The man looked at him in surprise. His surprise increased as the lad ran straight past him, pushing the large exit door open and slipping out into the night.

'Hey,' cried the porter, racing forward. 'Is that your son?' he asked the grizzled man.

''Course not,' came the stern reply.

'The little blighter,' said the porter with a twinkle of admiration in his eyes. He pushed open the door and glanced down the street. The boy had disappeared.

Peter had successfully escaped from the Nazi prison and was a free man again.

A large grin softened Peter's gaunt features. He was really pleased with himself. As he leaned over the parapet and stared at the seething, undulating waters of the Thames, he felt proud and happy. He had carried off his big adventure with great style. It was quite clear to him that when he grew up he would make a great secret agent.

Across the river he could see the flames of burning buildings after another night raid. The orange glow tinged the water so that it looked like blood. For some reason he thought of his mother. Her face, that bloated drunken face she'd had when last he saw her, came into his mind. It was strange that ever since he'd walked out on her, he hadn't given her one thought – until now. He felt himself weaken and tears began to brim up. He clenched his fists inside his pockets. He must not cry. Why should he cry? He felt nothing for her now. And yet something softened his resolve and the tears rolled down his cheeks. Whatever kind of cow she was, she was his mother. Without her, he had no one. And nowhere to go – except an orphanage. Well he bloody well wasn't going to one of those. He dragged his sleeve across his eyes and wiped the tears away. Feeling sorry for yourself is pointless. He had to be more practical than that. What would Tiger Blake do in his situation?

He didn't know. But the thought of Blake made him think of Johnny, Mr Hawke. And that thought warmed him. He remembered that night in his scruffy little flat when they'd had Spam and beans together and Johnny had given him the biggest portion. Peter grinned. Yeah, that was all right really. He was a good bloke and he'd been nice to him in the hospital. Although he hadn't turned up today. Well, Peter supposed, today wasn't over. He could be there now, staring at an empty bed with his arms filled with Tiger Blake comics, wondering where his young friend was. Really, he'd let Johnny down, not the other way around. That was twice he'd run away from him. He ought to explain and apologize. And maybe ... maybe Johnny Hawke could help him. Maybe.

thirty-three

Leo Epstein resisted the temptation to pour himself another whisky. He knew that he had to remain as sober as possible. Despite downing three glasses already, his mind was still clear and alert. Or so he thought. It seemed to him that the alcohol had had no effect on him whatsoever. It had failed to soften the edges of the real world, lulling him into a sense of warm security. He put this down to fear. He was frightened. Of course he was. He knew his life was in danger – John Hawke had convinced him of that. But what made the situation worse was that he didn't know exactly in what way. There was nothing tangible to prepare for or even run away from. Apparently he was next on the list of Pammie's lovers to be bumped off. But he wasn't about to place his life in the hands of a one-eyed amateur detective whose sole concern, it seemed to him, was to catch the killer. He was sure that Hawke saw him merely as a pawn in his game and the detective didn't give a damn what happened to Leo Epstein as long he got his man. That is why Epstein had left his office early, by the back entrance, and raced home to the safety of his flat. Here he had locked and chained the door and armed himself with his father's old army pistol. Let the bastard come now, he thought in a rare moment of bravado, I'm ready for him.

He sat in an armchair facing the door, with the gun resting on his lap. The room was in darkness, apart from a table lamp on the small table by his side.

As the evening wore on, he was not unaware of the irony of ignoring the air raid sirens, remaining holed up in his flat. Wasn't it more likely that he could end up dead in a bombing raid than being attacked by a murderer? Much more likely, in fact.

But still he stayed put. He liked the womb-like cosiness of his flat. With the heavy plush curtains, the bookcases and the tasteful works of art adorning the walls, it was his haven from the harsh world outside. It was his domain and if he were going to die, he'd rather do it here than out on the alien streets or in some cramped urine-smelling bomb shelter.

His flat had always been his escape from the sordid reality he was exposed to every day. As a solicitor he spent his time dealing with life's moral bankrupts and emotional cripples – the grubby flotsam and jetsam who lacked the ability and sense to organize their lives properly. On leaving the office every day, he felt unclean, tarnished by the work he was involved in. He was able to escape from all that, to cleanse himself here in the privacy of his own world. It's what kept him sane – that and a string of young girlfriends, his office girls usually, who provided the kind of uncomplicated sexual satisfaction that he desired. He felt nothing for these girls; they were just an attractive means to an end: the release of his sexual needs. That is until he met Pammie.

A cynical grin touched his lips as he thought of Pammie: her beautiful, provocative face, her lithe, yet womanly figure and those miraculous, sensuous eyes. On meeting her, the unthinkable happened. He fell in love. It was a new sensation to him. He had no notion that he was capable of the emotion so when it came, it was as though Pammie had released some internal floodgates. All the repressed passions held back for years – deliberately held back – flooded out and overnight, it seemed, he changed from being a self-sufficient being with total control of his own life to behaving like a moonstruck calf. He became obsessed with the girl and showered her with gifts and money in an attempt to make her his.

He was fully aware that she took advantage of his weakness for her, but he didn't care as long as she succumbed to him, went out with him, kissed him, let him hold her beneath the sheets and allowed him to make love to her. If money was the key which opened the door to this happiness, he didn't care. Buying happiness was not a new concept and he was lucky to have the means to do it.

He cast a wistful eye in the direction of his bedroom where they used to make love, spending long evenings in bed. He remembered the smoothness of her skin as he ran his fingers along her thigh and how he'd gently cup her breasts to kiss them while she moaned softly. Her responses to him were genuine; she did care for him. He was convinced of it. He had never known such bliss and now he was reminded with a desolate sadness, that he never would again.

Dammit, he would have another whisky. With an unsteady hand he splashed a generous measure into his glass. He closed his eyes and took a large gulp. He waited for the warming and relaxing effect that the single malt usually had upon his senses. He waited in vain. He was too tense, too focused on his fear and too miserable.

He allowed his fingers to run over the contours of the pistol. It was comforting to feel the cool metal, but he wondered whether he would have the nerve to use it? If this murdering madman broke in seeking some kind of revenge, could he fire the damned thing? He held the weapon and aimed it at the door, his finger closing tightly on the trigger. His hand began to shake. Christ, this was some sort of nightmare.

He dropped the weapon back in his lap and took another swig of whisky. He didn't know if he could shoot another human being until the moment arrived. How could he? It would be self defence, of course. He would be exonerated by the law, but would he be able to live with himself knowing that he had killed another person?

These are wandering thoughts, he told himself sharply. The whisky is starting work on my brain. He slammed the glass down on the table as an act of rejection. That was enough artificial stimulation.

And then something happened, something completely unexpected.

The doorbell rang.

Leo Epstein froze with fear.

thirty-four

Leo Epstein waited in a frozen panic. He had no idea what to do next. Perhaps, if he stayed put, whoever it was ringing his bell would go away. The logical part of his mind told him that no self-respecting murderer would actually ring the doorbell of his potential victim. They would just gain entry by either violent or surreptitious means and then carry out their work. But his racing heart and sweating palms were having none of this logic.

It came again – the soft ding dong chime. It resonated in the quiet apartment. His caller was persistent.

Epstein found his fingers curling around the cool, hard metal handle of the pistol. As he realized what he was doing, he recoiled in horror. His hand sprang free, releasing the gun. It dropped on to his lap and then slithered to the floor.

Now there came a knocking at the door, accompanied by a muffled voice calling his name and saying something that he could not hear clearly. He thought he heard the word 'death'.

He knew he had to respond. Like an arthritic marionette, he rose from the chair and slowly moved closer to the door. His gun lay untouched on the floor where it had fallen.

His visitor called out again and this time he could make out what the voice was saying. 'Mr Epstein, you've got to let me in. I need to speak to you. It's urgent. A matter of life and death.'

It was a woman's voice. Insistent but not hysterical.

Slowly he slipped back the bolt and released the Yale lock. Pulling the door ajar a few inches, he peered out into the corridor to catch sight of his visitor.

He recognized the woman immediately. What on earth was she doing here?

She stepped closer to the door until her face was barely a foot away from his.

'You've got to let me in, Mr Epstein. I just have to talk to you.'

'What about?'

Nervously, she looked up and down the corridor before replying. 'I can't talk about it out here but ...' – she lowered her voice to a whisper – 'I believe your life is in danger.'

'And you can help me?'

She nodded. 'I think I can.'

Without another word, Epstein held the door open enough to allow Freda Palfrey to enter.

Epstein felt tired, a little drunk and quite bewildered at the presence of Pammie's mother in his flat. He had no idea what she was there for.

'Do you want to sit down?'

She shook her head. That was fine by him. He really wanted to dispense with all formalities and discover the reason for this visit without delay.

'Now for Christ's sake tell me why you are here!' he demanded brusquely, running his fingers through his hair.

'I have something for you,' she said softly, fumbling in her handbag for a moment. She withdrew a dark shiny revolver and pointed it at Epstein. 'It's this,' she added, in the same calm even manner. 'I've come to kill you.'

'You ...' The word was virtually a croak, as Epstein staggered back in shock.

'Yes, me,' grinned Freda Palfrey. 'You are the last on my list of bastards who helped to destroy my angel Pamela.'

'You ... you've got me all wrong. I cared for Pammie. I loved her. I gave her things ... money.'

Freda Palfrey's eyes flickered with bleak amusement. 'Oh, yes, you gave her things. Why shouldn't you? She was a prostitute, after all. You bought her favours. You showed her that she could survive ... succeed by using her flesh as a commodity. The little girl I brought up as a sweet Christian angel was converted into a grubby tart by men like you. Your sort desecrates souls for cash. You cared nothing for her spiritual being ... you just wanted her body.'

'It ... it wasn't like that. I really did love Pammie. I would have married her....'

'But you didn't.'

'She wouldn't have me.'

'Of course not. She was too far down the road to corruption to save herself in the sanctity of marriage. We let our little girl into the world and men like you and Gordon Moore and Samuel Fraser destroyed her.'

Epstein, his brow now awash with perspiration, shook his head in panic. He was clear thinking enough to realize that he was dealing with a madwoman. Somehow he had to convince her that he was the innocent party in the perverted scenario which she had created for herself. It was possible that the grief she felt at the death of her daughter had tipped her into this crazy delusional state. It really didn't matter how or why but he realized if he didn't persuade her otherwise, he would end up as dead meat like Gordon Moore.

'If you really want someone to blame ... it's Samuel Fraser. He was her pimp. He lived off Pammie's earnings. He set her up as a ... as a prostitute. I only gave to her. I tried to make her happy.'

Freda Palfrey's careworn face relaxed into a cynical smile. 'I don't have to worry about Mr Fraser. The police have him. He'll swing and swing hard for Pamela's murder. And then he'll burn in Hell. What a bonfire that will be.'

Epstein realized that his cache of diversionary tactics was already empty. His brain searched desperately for another ploy to persuade this deranged creature not to shoot him.

'I can agree with you on that,' he said with some eagerness. 'Murder is a real sin. Fraser does deserve to die for killing Pammie.'

Freda Palfrey gave an unexpected chuckle. 'You think he

killed Pamela? Oh, no. He didn't kill Pamela.' She paused, her face now a stern, enigmatic mask. 'I did,' she said softly.

'You! You ... killed your own daughter?' Epstein shook his head in disbelief at this terrible revelation. The woman was seriously deranged. And yet as he gazed in horror at this gaunt woman, her fierce haunted eyes told him that she was telling him the truth.

'Yes, I killed Pamela. I had to. It was the only way to save her. What kind of mother would allow her little girl to carry on defiling her soul in such a manner? It had to stop. She didn't deserve to live. She had rejected decency and morality for a filthy, corrupt way of living and therefore had forfeited her right to life. She is much better off dead.'

Epstein felt sick at heart and slumped down into his chair. He couldn't fully believe this living nightmare in which he was taking part. He wanted to close his eyes in the hope that it would all disappear.

But he knew it wouldn't. He was here in the room with a crazy woman who had killed the only girl he had ever really cared for and was now about to end his life as well. That was his new, dark reality.

'How could ... how could you do that to your own flesh and blood?' he asked. 'She was your daughter, for God's sake.'

'Yes she was and that's why I took mercy on her and ended her foul existence.'

'She needed love and understanding not a damned bullet.'

Freda Palfrey blanched with anger at this remark and shook the pistol at Epstein. 'Do you think it was easy? Do you think I was happy to do it? I sobbed myself to sleep for weeks when I knew that this was the only answer. It was only the fact that I was right and God was on my side that gave me the courage to do it. The little girl I brought into the world, that sweet innocent child had become a sinful monster. I have no conscience about the matter. It was the right thing to do.'

Epstein shook his head in disbelief. 'I don't understand ... I just don't understand.' His bewilderment seemed to amuse her.

Out of the corner of his eye, he noticed his discarded pistol near his feet. He was fairly certain Mrs Palfrey hadn't seen it. Could he make a grab for it and defend himself? He quickly weighed up the situation and realized that by the time he had snatched up the weapon, she would have shot him.

'Bastards like you never do understand. You go through life without a thought for the people you use, people you taint with your money.'

'What on earth are you going to do? Go after every man who slept with Pammie and kill them? It's quite a long list.'

Freda Palfrey's face twisted with anger. 'I know. Don't you think I know? I knew all about my daughter. She thought she had kept her "other" life a secret, her life away from home, but she hadn't. Not from me anyway. Right from the beginning, I followed her. Watched her. Saw what she was getting up to. I was her guardian angel.'

Epstein could imagine the manic vigilance with which she had spied on her daughter. In his conversations with Pammie, she had always avoided talking about her home life but he had deduced that she had led a repressed existence there and was delighted when she was able to move into a place of her own. In the early days, when she first came to work for him, he had witnessed the joy and glee she exhibited at the simplest of treats. It was as though she had been kept cocooned – kept away from the real world. Epstein saw now that this was indeed the case. The mother had been unable to sever the umbilical cord. And Pammie's repression had built within her an enormous appetite for life, an appetite which knew no moral boundaries. She had become the person she was because of the way she had been treated at home. Epstein could see that Freda Palfrey had gone beyond being convinced that this was the truth of the situation. She had obviously been obsessed with 'protecting' her daughter for such a long time and this obsession had led to insanity. And there was no reasoning with an insane woman, especially when she had gun.

'I knew I could only destroy a small number of those men

who helped to bring about her downfall. I did not have to think for too long who I wanted to kill. There was Fraser, Moore and you. Fraser, because he really used my girl; you called him a pimp and that's right. Pamela was little more than a business asset to him.

'Gordon Moore, because he was famous and had money and he used his wealth and fame to get him whatever he wanted. And you, Mr Leo Epstein, because you took advantage of Pamela's innocence. When she came to work for you, she knew nothing of sex or loose morals, but under your guidance she soon learned. And now you make it worse by saying that you cared for her! You liar! You have even deceived yourself. Like all men ... like all men the only thing you care about is you.'

She was now roaring her words now, her whole body trembling with fury. Epstein jumped to his feet. He couldn't just wait there to be shot like some kind of diseased animal. He had to take some action. If he moved swiftly, dropping to the ground, and lunging forward he might be able to overpower her in a rugby tackle. It was very risky, but what was the alternative? Remain where he was like a sitting duck and get the full blast in his chest?

But before he could make a move, Freda Palfrey cocked the pistol.

'No!' he cried and leapt forward. As he did so, a shot rang out.

thirty-five

My pal Leo Epstein lived in a select part of Holborn. Cedar Court was a prestigious-looking block of flats which appeared from its grey stone and angular appearance as though it had been built less than ten years ago. There was obviously money to be made in the solicitoring game.

Leaving my rather wobbly bike at the gateway, I passed through the grand revolving doors into the entrance hall, which was guarded in a somewhat incompetent fashion by a slumbering doorman. I slipped by the dozing fellow and made my way up in the lift to the third floor. Distractedly, I stared at the shaking gates of the lift as I rattled upwards to the appointed floor and I grew very nervous. While pedalling here as though all the devils in hell and a troop of Gestapo thugs had been on my tail, I hadn't really thought about what I was likely to encounter once I had actually reached Epstein's apartment. A corpse possibly? Or just a frightened man hiding in the bathroom? Or maybe a couple copulating in bed? Well, that would be a relief!

I reached the third floor and sought out Flat 14. The corridor was empty and so I pulled my pistol from my raincoat pocket. It was, I knew, an overly dramatic gesture but I reckoned I would need the gun. I hated the things. I wasn't a naturally violent man, although I could look after myself in a scrap, but guns gave one a kind of unfair advantage. And, as I clasped the handle firmly, I could not forget what one of its bigger brothers had done to me.

I was unsure whether to ring the bell or just try to enter Epstein's apartment without announcing my presence. Such a choice was wrested from me for, as I stood before the door, I heard a shot ring out inside, followed by a sharp cry.

Without hesitation I burst through the door, to catch sight of Epstein lying on the floor, his right hand clutching his left shoulder. Rivulets of blood were running through his fingers on to his shirt. Standing over him was a dark shape. The shape had a gun. At the sound of my noisy entrance, the shape turned in my direction. It was Freda Palfrey. My brain fizzed and crackled. In an instant I understood.

The jigsaw was complete.

It was the mother – not the father. Of course. I had so convinced myself that Eric Palfrey was the killer, I had never placed his wife anywhere near the frame. How naïve was that?

However, I had no time to develop these thoughts at that moment for now she was pointing her gun at me. My instinct was to fire at her before she had a chance to pull the trigger, but I couldn't. How could I shoot this woman, deranged as she was? Some inbuilt instinct held me back from shooting. And yet, Johnny Boy, my brain screamed, you just can't stand there and let her blast you to kingdom come. Do something, you fool! So I did. In desperation, I *threw* my gun at her. With great force and reasonable accuracy.

Freda Palfrey screamed as it thudded against her chest.

Distracted by the flying weapon, she staggered backwards and then stumbled sideways with the shock. I rushed forward and knocked her gun flying from her hand. She let out another scream. 'You devil,' she cried and tried to attack me, but I held her arms at bay. She struggled for a while, her fingers wriggling desperately to reach my face, but she had little strength and soon collapsed on the floor in a sobbing heap.

Epstein pulled himself up into a sitting position. 'She tried to kill me,' he bleated, still clutching his wounded shoulder.

'You were the lucky one,' I said, picking up the telephone.

Two hours later I was sitting in the back of a police car hurtling through the darkened streets of London on the way to the

Palfreys house in Pinner. Sitting beside me was my old mate Inspector David Llewellyn. It was he I telephoned from Epstein's flat and he had set official things in motion. The injured solicitor was scooped up and taken to hospital to have his wound attended to. I estimated that a long wait was in store for Mr Epstein. After a night of heavy bombing, the casualties would be numerous and a poncey solicitor who'd been involved in a domestic shooting would come well down the list of priorities.

Freda Palfrey had been carted off to the cells. She went quietly, with barely a word, her face revealing none of her feelings or inner turmoil. It was as though all her emotions had been squeezed out of her.

David was chuckling by the side of me as the car rocked gently from side to side as it sped down the narrow streets. 'Old Dirty Knight won't like this at all,' he said with some delight. 'He was convinced that Fraser was the guilty party....'

'Or had convinced himself that was the truth,' I ventured.

David nodded. 'You are probably right. In essence he's a good copper, but he does tend to jump to conclusions and then refuses to budge.' He chuckled again. 'He'll hate you even more now you've proved him wrong.'

'I'm not sure I've proved anything. I am as surprised as anyone that Mrs Palfrey is our man ... so to speak.'

'Right you are. A real turn up for the book. Still, she's not right in the head, is she?'

'Not now, I suppose. An obsessive mother unable to cut the apron strings ... I can't help but feel sorry for her.'

'Come on, boy, she was not that innocent. She was a cunning old girl and everything was coldly premeditated.'

'But her actions were selfless. She was saving her daughter and punishing her corrupters.'

'Saving her daughter ...? By stabbing her in the chest? I can't cope with that kind of twisted psychology.'

'If it's any consolation, I don't understand it fully myself,' I said, lighting up a cigarette. While waiting for the ambulance

Epstein had told me in great detail about her visit to his flat and all that she had said to him, had confessed to him. Freda Palfrey had just sat there listening to his recital and never said a word. Her face was a blank sheet registering no emotion. In fact, I wondered if she was actually listening to him. Probably not. She was most likely lost in some other world where her kind of justice made sense.

'Do you think the father was in on it?' asked David.

I shook my head. 'I don't think so. If they were both involved, why on earth come to me to investigate the matter?'

'People who are not right in the head do many strange things.'

I blew a wreath of grey smoke at my own reflection in the darkened window of the car. 'No, I think he was as naïve and innocent as the rest of us. He loved Pammie too much to hurt her in that way. I wonder how he'll take it.'

'Well, we'll soon know,' David observed, as the patrol car pulled up outside the Palfrey home. Not much of a home now.

I glanced at my watch. It was just coming up to 2 a.m. My God, I thought, what a long night it's been.

David instructed the driver to stay in the car, while we went to rouse Mr Palfrey. I did not envy David's job of passing on the terrible news that his wife was in custody on the charge of murder and that one of the victims was his daughter.

He wrapped hard on the front door and rang the bell. We heard the notes of 'Greensleeves' playing faintly. We waited. There was no response. With the blackout curtains, it was almost impossible to tell whether anyone had been roused by the noise. David tried again, shouting the word, 'Police' through the letter box.

Nothing.

He gave me a quizzical look. 'Not happy about this. Reckon I'll have to make a forced entry.'

I nodded and placed a hand on his shoulder. 'Well, before you do yourself some personal injury trying to break the door down, let me have a go with my portable burgling kit,' I said, taking out my sturdy bit of wire.

In less than two minutes I had released the lock and we were able to enter the Palfrey household. The first thing we became aware of was a smell, faint but definite.

'Gas,' I said.

'Bloody right,' he cried, opening the first door he came to – the one leading to the sitting-room. He had difficulty pushing the door back because something was obstructing it: a row of cushions.

The smell of gas grew stronger. The room was full of it.

'Don't, for God's sake, turn the light on,' I cried. 'One spark and we could be up there with the Spitfires.'

'I'll use my torch. I'll go outside to switch it on.'

This done, we both clamped out handkerchiefs to our faces and peered inside the room. The beam of David's torch soon fell upon the body of Eric Palfrey; he was lying by the gas fire, his head resting on a cushion. The unlit fire hissed gas at us.

I tackled the gas fire, switching it off, while David pulled back the blackout curtains and threw open the windows. For a while we both stood with our heads outside the windows breathing deeply, filling our lungs with untainted cold night air. After ten minutes or so, the atmosphere had cleared in the room sufficiently for us to lift the body and carry it into the hallway and then out on to the path outside. Of course, it was too late. Eric Palfrey was dead. No doubt it was what he had wanted: to float to his Maker on a sea of fumed sleep.

In his hand he clutched a piece of paper. Gently I unfolded his fingers back and released it.

The paper contained just two words. 'I know.'

thirty-six

Dawn was creeping into the sky when a police car dropped me off at the corner of Oxford Street and Tottenham Court Road. I thanked the driver for the lift. He gave me a weary look to indicate that he was only obeying orders and that he'd had no choice in the matter. I had hardly stepped out of the vehicle when he slammed it into gear and with a squeal of tyres he drove off at speed.

For some time I watched the car, its tail lights flashing angrily occasionally as the tired driver braked for some reason or other, until it had disappeared from sight – and I was alone. A solitary figure in a lonely landscape. The shapes of clouds could now be discerned overhead, but the lightening sky showed no traces of blue. It was to be another grey day. In more ways than one.

As I began to trudge back to my flat, I felt an overwhelming sense of sadness and emptiness. In many ways, I had only been a peripheral player in the Palfrey tragedy but events had affected me more than I could articulate. A family had destroyed itself for no real reason. And there were other casualties as well. With a measure of tolerance, understanding and some undemanding love, none of this would have happened.

I shrugged. What did I know? I was just the poor bastard who'd tried to untie the knots in this bloody ball of string. I had failed. Well, all but. I reckoned I might get a Christmas card from Leo Epstein. I grinned weakly at the thought.

I spotted an empty milk bottle in the gutter and for no explainable reason I stepped into the kerb and gave it a hearty kick. It sailed into the air and landed in the middle of the road where it smashed into a thousand pieces. It gave me great satisfaction to see the shiny fragments scatter across the tarmac. It lightened my soul.

As I got to the corner of Priors Court, I passed Sammy Wills with his milk cart. I patted his horse, Marcel, and blagged a free pint of milk from Sammy.

'Don't drink it all at once, Master Johnny,' said old Sammy, giving me his toothless grin.

'This has to last me the week,' I called back over my shoulder.

'Away with you,' he called, pulling his old nag further down the street.

When I arrived at the entrance to Hawke Towers, I found it blocked by a bundle of rags – or what at first glance appeared to be a bundle of rags. It was in fact a little boy, curled in a foetal position, fast asleep. *Déjà vu* time.

It was Peter.

I roused him gently, tugging his shoulder until his eyes flickered open. It took him a while to remember who he was, where he was and who the chap was louring over him. When he did, his face brightened and his eyes shone. 'Johnny ... Mr Hawke. You've come at last.'

'What on earth are you doing here, my lad?'

'I've come to stay with you, of course. I've left the hospital. I'm better now. The nurse told me. And she said that they were going to send me to an orphanage. That's why I had to escape. Well, I'm not going to one of them prisons. You won't let them take me, will you?'

He suddenly lunged forward and clasped his arms around my legs and began to sob.

God, I thought, this long, horrible night is still not over.

'I think,' I said, at length, 'we'd better go in for some breakfast.'

His wet, tearstained face gazed up at me. 'Oh, yes please,' he grinned.

*

As usual the Hawke larder yielded up little of consequence. I managed to find a few slices of bread and a tin of beans. Well, beans on stale unbuttered bread was a speciality of the house. However, it delighted Peter. He sat enraptured, watching me while I prepared this modest feast and then he wolfed it down as though he hadn't eaten for months.

I poured us both a mug of tea. He slurped his noisily and then apologized.

'Now then,' I said as casually as possible, 'what's all this about you leaving the hospital ... and the truth mind. Remember Tiger Blake never lies.'

'Except to the enemy.'

'Well, that's different. And I'm your friend.'

Peter grinned and nodded. 'Yes,' he said.

And so he told me all about his daring 'escape' from the clutches of his enemies at the hospital who planned to cart him off to an orphanage prison; and how he reckoned I would let him stay with me instead, 'kind of adopting me, sort of' because he liked me and we both liked Tiger Blake.

Looking at that smiling little boy, with the animated features and the bright light of hope burning fiercely in his eyes, I felt sick at heart. I wanted to hold him to my breast and hug him tightly until all his demons, all his unhappiness had been squeezed away.

But I couldn't do that. It wouldn't work. Life is not that easy.

'Well, we'll have to see, Peter, old chap. Certainly for the moment you can call Hawke Towers your home,' I said as casually as possible, playing for time with a false smile in place.

That lie seemed to please him and he began slurping his tea once more.

'One thing, Peter ... you mustn't run away from me again. OK? Cross your heart and hope to die.'

'It's a deal: cross my heart and hope to die.'

And then another slurp.

*

After the food and the warm tea, I was overcome with tired-ness. Luckily so was my young charge and almost in unison, we fell into a deep sleep in our chairs by the fireplace like two old duffers in a gentleman's club after one snifter of brandy too much.

Pressure on my bladder roused me first and I was amused to hear my young guest giving forth a whole series of variegated pig-like snores.

I gave myself a strip wash, shaved and dug out a clean shirt from the wardrobe. I felt almost human again. While I was doing this, Peter snored on as though giving an inarticulate commentary to my actions. When I was ready, I woke the lad.

'I've got to go out now. I've a few jobs need doing. I want you to be a good fellow and wait here for me. I'll be back before dark. OK?'

Bleary-eyed, he nodded.

'If you get hungry there's a packet of biscuits in that cupboard. And you know how to make a cup of tea, I'm sure. When I get back, I'll take you out for a meal at a very posh restaurant, I know.'

'Really?'

'Really. There are some Tiger Blake comics I got you under that chair so you can spend some time reading them.'

'Great. Thanks, Johnny.'

I ruffled his hair. 'That's OK, kid.'

He grinned back at me. I had never seen him so happy.

thirty-seven

When I entered the cell, Freda Palfrey was sitting on the bed, a tray with an uneaten meal by her side. She was staring straight ahead at some invisible point beyond the confines of her prison, her hands clasped together on her lap.

Her eyes flickered with recognition as I pulled up a chair and sat opposite her.

'Hello, Mrs Palfrey,' I said, quietly.

She did not reply.

'You'll forgive me for coming to see you, but there are some things that are nagging at the back of my brain – some things I've got to understand. Things that only you can tell me.'

She turned to look at me. 'Me?' she said softly with some puzzlement.

I nodded. 'It might help you to talk.'

She shook her head. 'I've done with talking.'

'The police will have other ideas. But their purpose is not mine.'

She raised her eyebrows.

'I just need to know the truth ... to lend you a sympathetic ear.'

She paused for a while.

'I am not in need of sympathy.'

She meant it.

I tried a different approach. 'Why did you engage me to find your daughter when you knew where she was all the time? You did know where she was, didn't you?'

Her features registered no emotion but her eyes flickered with amusement. 'Oh, yes, I knew. As soon as Pamela started to work for Epstein, I made it my business to keep an eye on her. She was my baby and she didn't know the nastiness of the world. Father and I had done our best to protect her from it. But we couldn't keep her at home for ever. So I watched her, followed her, and saw, to my horror, what she was turning in to. She became a tramp, a cheap whore. Years of our care, training and preaching were dispensed with overnight. It was as though she had flung our love and moral values back in our faces. It was then that I knew I had to kill her. To save her soul.' She paused and allowed herself a little ironic smile. 'But of course I can't expect you to understand.'

I shook my head. 'No, you're right, I don't understand.'

'Of course I had to bide my time. Choose the right moment to release my Pamela from her sordid existence. But then events overtook me. You see I never told Father what our daughter had become. It would have destroyed him. He just thought she had rebelled a little, that's all. He was desperate to find her. He was sure he could persuade her to come home again.'

'And that's why you came to me.'

She nodded. 'I had to. At first Father wanted to go to the police but I managed to persuade him to employ a private detective instead. I told him that after all it was a personal, domestic matter. There was no crime involved. So he agreed. I picked your name out of the phone book.' She turned her stony gaze towards me. 'I didn't expect you to be very good.'

I raised a laconic eyebrow.

'But as soon as I met you, I knew. I knew that you'd find Pamela pretty quickly and so my time was limited....' Her words faltered and she turned away from me.

'You had to kill her before I found her.'

There was no reply. The silence said it all.

'My God,' I said, a thought striking me, 'so it was you, it was you who hit me from behind. You almost killed me.'

'I didn't intend you to die. I just wanted ... I was just trying to buy myself some time.'

I leaned forward and put my hand on her shoulder. Freda Palfrey stiffened, her whole body turning rigid.

'Didn't you think to talk to her? Find out why she was acting the way she was? Maybe try to understand her. Persuade her to come home?'

'It was too late,' she cried, the words echoing around the small cell. 'She was a whore. That's all there is to it.'

There was no breaking through that armour of self-conviction that Freda Palfrey had constructed for herself. It had given her strength, determination and power and in the final months of her life it would give her faith. But she was wrong. Whatever self-righteous impulse or belief drove her to plunge the knife in to her own daughter's chest did not alter that fact. She had committed murder.

Suddenly I felt weary and eager to leave. I had learned perhaps more than I needed or wanted to know. Sad though this creature was, there was something repellent about her, too. It seemed that she had subjugated all her human and motherly feelings to carry out this crazy act of murder.

As I rose to go she turned to me again. 'I *did* talk to her,' she said softly, almost to herself. 'That night I went to her flat. I told her of all the heinous things she'd done. How she had blackened her soul though her own selfish desires. I told her the truth. Do you know what she did? She laughed at me. Just laughed. She said I was pathetic ... my own daughter. And she laughed. I knew then there was no going back. I did the right thing.'

I shook my head. 'It is not given to us to have the power to decide such things ... to take the law into our own hands. It is a transgression.'

'I can live with my conscience for the short span I have left.'

I reached the door. 'I wonder. You didn't know that Pamela was pregnant did you?'

Her eyes widened in horror. Silently, she mouthed the word 'pregnant' as she stared at me in disbelief.

I nodded. 'Yes. She was expecting a baby. Your grandchild.'

It was a few seconds before the truth sank in and then Freda Palfrey threw back her head in a roaring wail of despair. It rang in my ears long after I had left the cell.

For some time I walked along the embankment, kicking the errant piles of autumn leaves which had collected there, trying to expunge all the disturbing memories of the Palfrey case from my mind without much success. They seemed embedded in my consciousness like the fragments of some unpleasant dream which refused to fade away. In particular I was reminded of the bloodstained mattress and Freda Palfrey's feral cry of anguish as she learned that Pamela was expecting a baby.

After a while I leaned over the parapet, lit a Craven A and watched the grey water swirl past sluggishly. As I gazed, mesmerized almost by the seething, truculent river, I realized that I was putting off another unpleasant duty that had come along with the case.

I sighed, flicked the tab end into the river, and set forth for Charing Cross Hospital.

On reaching the children's ward I asked to speak to Nurse McAndrew. My luck was in. She had just come on duty.

'Have you heard the news?' she said, without any preliminary greeting, bundling me into an empty side ward.

'News?'

'About Peter. He's done a bunk. Ran away last night.'

I couldn't help but smile at the phrase 'done a bunk'. It brought to mind an image of Peter, pretending to be Tiger Blake affecting an escape from the Hospital Prisoner of War Camp.

'What's so funny?' Sister McAndrew was obviously dismayed and annoyed at my reaction.

'He's with me,' I said, still grinning.

'With you!'

I held up my hands in defence. 'I had nothing to do with it. The lad just took it into his head to jump ship and come to live with me. I found him on my doorstep early this morning when I got in.'

'The poor mite.'

'It seems he thinks I'm a better bet than an orphanage.'

'But he can't live with you!'

'I know. But he can't go to a bloody orphanage either. I speak from experience.'

'I see.'

'Those places crush you. Stamp out any spark of individuality. They crucify sensitive souls like Peter.'

'Sensitive souls like you?' It was Sister Susan McAndrew's turn to smile.

'I suppose,' I replied, with a somewhat sheepish grin.

'I think I've got the answer. I've been on the phone to my sister, Julia: she's married to a farmer in Devon. They're very happy to take Peter on as an evacuee for the duration.'

'That's wonderful,' I beamed. 'All the lad needs is a loving stable home life.'

'And after the war ... what then?'

'We'll cross that bridge when we come to it, Auntie Susan.'

We laughed. It was a warm, happy laugh which made us feel good.

'I'll need to deal with the paperwork and stuff, but I'm sure I'll be able to sort it out without much difficulty. Kids are a nuisance in London. They're being shipped to the country by the cartload. One more poor sod won't make much difference.'

'Nurse McAndrew, I love you,' I beamed, and embraced her, giving her a kiss on the lips.

She blushed and, pulling away from me, she adjusted her cap.

'If that's a proposal, the answer is no,' she said, with a twinkle in her eye.

An hour later I was on my third errand of the day. I stood once more before the shabby terraced house in Carlton Street in Maida Vale. The curtains were drawn and there was no sign of life. I gazed at the house for some time wondering whether to knock or not when the door of the adjoining property opened abruptly and an aged, thin-faced old crone appeared on the doorstep. Although it was the afternoon, she was wearing a faded dressing-gown wrapped around her scraggy frame. Her hair was in curlers and a smoking cigarette dangled precariously from her lip.

'If you're looking for that young couple what live there, you're out of luck, mister.'

'Why's that?' I asked simply.

'They've moved out. Did a moonlight flit last night. Saw 'em with my own eyes. You a debt collector? Reckon you've missed the boat with them two.' She gave a strangled rasp which I assumed was an expression of merriment but it soon developed into a hacking cough.

I raised my hat in a polite gesture, thanked the old witch for the information she had proffered and turned on my heel.

'Goodbye, Eve,' I muttered under my breath, as I trundled back to Warwick Street tube station. 'I hope you'll be all right.'

thirty-eight

That evening I took Peter for the promised slap-up meal in a posh restaurant. Well, at least we had the best table at Benny's Café. And this was certainly a notch up on the doorways that the lad had been used to recently. With a little hint from me Benny made an effort to make the occasion special. He even lit a candle on the table to help create a festive effect. I was determined that neither beans nor Spam would be a feature of our little repast and Benny rose to the culinary challenge providing us with two steaming plates of spaghetti bolognaise. Remarkably, the bolognaise had a passing resemblance to beef. A first for Benny.

Peter was delighted with the experience and giggled heartily as he sucked hard on the long strands of spaghetti until they shot into his mouth with some force, leaving the surrounding area smeared with bolognaise sauce. Benny hovered by our table, a jovial spectre at the feast, happy that his meal was causing so much enjoyment.

As he cleared our plates away, he leaned forward in a conspiratorial fashion. 'In honour of our young guest this evening, I think I can rustle up some ice-cream if that would be acceptable.'

'Would you like some ice-cream, Peter?' I asked.

He beamed and nodded. 'Yes, please.'

Benny beamed too. 'On the house,' he crowed, as he disappeared into the kitchen.

'This is great,' said Peter, his face flushed with pleasure.

'Only the best for my little friend.'

His hand stole across the table and touched mine. 'We are friends, Johnny, aren't we?'

'Certainly are. Whatever happens.'

'Whatever happens? What d'you mean?'

'I've got some news for you.'

The smile faded from Peter's face.

I ruffled his hair. 'It's good news.'

At this point Benny plonked a dish of ice-cream in front of him. 'Enjoy, my boy,' he grinned.

'What about me?' I asked.

'Ice-cream is for the children, Johnny. Special treat. For you, I got a custard pie....'

'I'll pass on that.'

Benny gave a mock grunt of disdain and shuffled off.

'What news?' asked Peter when Benny had left us, his dish of ice-cream untouched.

'I've found a home for you ... in the countryside away from all the bombing.'

'A home?'

'Yes. Not an orphanage but a proper home with two kind people who'll sort of be your mum and dad for a while. Until we beat the Germans.'

'Will you be there?'

I shook my head. 'My work is in London. But I'll come down and see you. And I'll write and send you some Tiger Blake comics.'

'Do you promise? Please promise.'

'Of course. I'm not losing touch with you, you little rascal. We're pals, aren't we?'

Peter nodded vigorously, his smile forming again.

'Now eat your ice-cream before it melts.'

Peter nodded and tucked in. After a few mouthfuls, he passed the spoon to me. 'You have some, too,' he said with a smile.

A few days later with Peter clutching my hand we entered the stately portals of Paddington Station. It was just before midday and it was heaving with travellers. As we pushed through the crowds, Susan McAndrew came forward to greet us. She bent down and gave Peter a hug. He glanced up at me, embarrassed. I knew he liked Susan but this show of affection from a lady affected his masculine image. I gave him a knowing look.

Susan had secured some leave and was taking Peter down to her sister's farm in Devon to help settle Peter in.

'Our train's arrived. It's on platform five,' she cried above the hubbub.

I nodded and together we made our way there, each holding Peter by the hand, looking for all the world like a pair of devoted parents.

Peter and Susan boarded the train and leaned out of the carriage door window.

'Oh,' I cried, 'just before I forget.' I pulled some comics from the inside of my coat and passed them over to Peter. 'Something for you to read on the train.'

His little face crumpled and he began to cry. 'Can't you come with us?'

For one reckless moment I almost said yes but I didn't. I shook my head instead. 'I've got some important business to deal with here in London. You've got my address. Don't forget to write. And I'll come down and see you very soon.'

He nodded bravely, brushing the tears from his eyes.

I leaned closer to him. 'Now, remember, there may be Nazi spies on the train, so keep your eyes open. It's your mission to protect Nurse McAndrew.'

Peter looked at me seriously and rose to his full height. 'You can rely on me, Johnny.'

'Good man.'

The whistle blew and the train began to move. We were all lost for words now and all we could do was wave at each other. And so I waved until the train shimmered out of sight.